Through The Tears

By

Nadia Cenci and Stella Lever

Acknowledgements;

To our husbands, Steve and Mark for their continuous encouragement and support.

To Leon Maculewicz, for the wonderful graphics and his enthusiasm.

ISBN 978-1-4116-8845-2

In loving
memory of our
dear dads

Des Cenci and Tim Spindler

PART ONE

THE
TEARS

CHAPTER 1

Gina walked slowly towards home, her steps small and hesitant. The pouring rain felt comforting somehow, reflecting the emptiness that she felt inside and the feeling of anxiety as she made her way towards the inevitable. Gina turned into the street, not daring to look up and check if the lights were on – that Joe had arrived home. She pushed her red curly hair away from her wet cheeks and slowly lifted her head. The rain momentarily blurred her vision as she looked into the distance, scrunching her eyes to focus on the house at the end of the street. Her heart missed a beat – the hall and bedroom lights were glaring out.

Gina Harper had gone out that evening without telling her husband. Going out was a rare occasion in itself, but not telling Joe her exact whereabouts was unique. Claire, her best friend, had reached the ripe-old age of thirty and that night had again begged Gina to help celebrate the end of an era. Gina had initially declined the invitation, promising to make up for it some other way, as she knew that Joe would sulk like a baby for a whole week before the event and, at best, keep it up for several days afterwards. As luck would have it though, Joe had decided that he deserved a Friday night out with the lads after a hard week at work and had set off without any tea. Gina's mother had gladly offered to look after Kieran overnight and had told her to go out and have some fun. She smiled as she thought of her beautiful five-year old, with his black curly hair, dark brown eyes and olive skin. Kieran, always ready with a captivating smile and totally oblivious, or so she hoped, of the threat to his own stable environment. He was the reason that Gina had to make this marriage work as best she could, whatever her own sacrifices, but for the moment she needed to take her mother's advice and enjoy her own time. And that is exactly what she had done – had some fun, yes fun, for a change.

'Why shouldn't I'? she thought to herself.

Perhaps he had gone to bed and crashed out in a drunken stupor before realising she was not there? Perhaps she had left the lights on, in her rush to join the party? No, Gina was certain that these were remote scenarios and sighed. She wished she had come home sooner but the time had just flown by and now there was no choice but to face the music, explaining the last minute arrangement.

Suddenly angry at the turmoil he always inflicted on her daily life, Gina's steps became determined and purposeful as she made her way up the path to the front door. The empty milk bottles outside were broken and scattered over a small area, along with bits of old bus tickets and a few copper coins. There was no sound coming from inside as she put the key in the lock and turned it. Gina held her breath, as if the sound of her breathing might wake him. As she opened the door wider, Gina felt a presence at the top of the hall stairs. She looked up to see Joe staring down at her, his eyes filled with hatred. His cold, cold, blue questioning eyes. Just staring.

'Oh shit,' Gina whispered. The determination previously reflected in her expressive brown eyes was beginning to wither. Her head started to pound as the rising fear reached down to the pit of her stomach. From the corner of her eye, she saw something glinting on the floor of the lounge. Her eyes darted involuntarily back and forth until they rested on the object that had seized her attention. The hall light reflected on its long shape. It was a knife – a kitchen knife which had been stabbed into the carpet and stood upright – a message from Joe which paralysed her with fear.

Gina looked up at Joe, who was swaying from side to side, his cold eyes reflecting his utter disgust of, what he thought to be her unforgivable behaviour.

'Oh my God Joe, not again, please,' she begged.

As Joe leapt forward, missing his footing, Gina took the opportunity to run out, to run away from the nightmare that was to come.

'You fucking bitch. You whore. Where the fuck have you been?' His contorted face screamed as he lurched after her, finally catching up as she tried to reach her neighbour's house. Joe grabbed her by the hair and dragged her backwards along the pavement. Gina could feel clumps of her hair being ripped from her head as she tried to stay upright to minimise the pain. Her stiletto heels were slipping against the wet pavement, so she twisted her body to face forwards in an effort to free herself from his determined grasp. But there was no chance of escape when Joe pulled her by the left arm and grabbed the back of her neck so tightly that she could feel the pain shoot down her shoulders. Gina screamed and cried for help as she pushed against the doorframe to avoid being shut off from anyone willing to help. Her bid for rescue was thwarted as he pushed her into the hallway and onto the floor. The neighbour's curtains twitched and a concerned face peeped out, looked around the front garden, and then disappeared back into the shadows.

CHAPTER 2

Kate tensed indefinably in her chair. She reached forward and lit another cigarette as her thoughts crystallised and she finally concluded what she must do. When he did finally walk through that door she would confront him; she couldn't go on like this.

Earlier that evening Kate had arrived home to an empty house. After preparing a sandwich which lay half eaten and curled up on the coffee table, she had marked 3B's essays and then prepared next week's lesson plans. By then Geoffrey had still not arrived home so she turned on the television but immediately pressed the mute button as the noise interrupted her thoughts. She often did this as she couldn't bear a blank television screen. It reminded her too much of Orwell's Big Brother – that blank grey eye staring out at her, mirroring her own expression as she stared back at it. So, while some inane light entertainment scheduling had flickered silently at her, trying to attract her attention, Kate had spent the last few hours looking blankly at it as she wondered what had gone so badly wrong. In the beginning it had been so right, a wonderful physical passion cementing a loving, emotional and spiritual relationship. Their mutual respect for each other's intellectual prowess had filled their conversations with discussions about everything from politics and religion to what colour and style to decorate the bedroom. When they weren't earning their living they were together, just enjoying each other's company.

But it had all gone wrong. When? Was it last autumn when Kate fell pregnant and after much cajoling from Geoffrey about how the time wasn't right as they didn't have enough money and he wanted everything perfect for her for their first born, she had reluctantly agreed to an abortion? No. The rot had begun to set in before then. But over the following winter and spring it had got worse – much worse. It was now so bad that when he was at home she felt more isolated and lonely than she did when she was sitting at home alone. They existed through entire evenings without talking to or looking at each other. But it wasn't that comfortable silence you have with someone you are at one with – quite the contrary. It was so uncomfortable that she was constantly aware of his presence just outside of her line of vision and acutely aware of any slight movement she herself made.

Her myriad thoughts finally fell into coherent order. Things had got to the stage where they couldn't go on. She had to confront him; they had to do something about their situation; they had to try to recapture those early years before it was too late.

It was after midnight – where was he? Even if he had gone to the pub for a drink after work with his colleagues and stayed until closing time, he would have been home by now. Was he avoiding her, hoping she'd have gone to bed before he came in? She often did, just to avoid him.

Just then his key turned in the lock and every nerve and muscle in her body tensed. Stay focused, get your points across calmly, don't shout or rant and rave, but most of all – don't cry! He walked in and his face dropped when he saw her sitting there.

'I'm going straight to bed, I'm knackered,' he snapped at her with a visible sneer that contorted his dark, weathered features into ugliness.

'No Geoffrey, please, we need to talk. We can't go on like this.'

'Yes, you're right,' he paused, only for a split second, but it seemed to last forever. 'I want out!'

Her thoughts went into overdrive. No, this isn't what she wanted. She didn't want it to end; she wanted it to go back to how it used to be. They had had something so good, if only they were to try harder they could get it back again. She felt the tears prick her eyes. She fumbled for her words and finally blurted out a muffled 'Why?'

'You've just said it. We can't go on like this. There's nothing left between us and we're suffocating each other. Give me a few days to sort myself out, to find somewhere else to live and I'll move out. Until then I'll sleep in the spare room.'

His cold, calculating and so matter of fact reply was harsh even by his standards, and it cut her to the core. 'But I thought we could talk through our problems, try to work things out, give it another go.'

'No,' he interrupted brusquely. 'It wouldn't work. It might for a few weeks, but it would revert back. Besides, it's gone too far for that.'

She started to cry, but instead of the comforting arm around her, that most men with just an ounce of compassion would have given, he merely said, 'I'm off to bed so I suggest you get some sleep as well, and tomorrow we can sort out the details.' With that he walked upstairs.

Kate sat there motionless, tears silently cascading down her face, despite her feeling painfully numb. Her head was so full of thoughts and yet so empty. She wished she hadn't said anything but she had – and there was no turning back. She knew he'd try to sneak away tomorrow morning before she'd got up, he'd run away as he always did, not wanting to sort things out properly. But she'd fox him; she wouldn't go to bed; she'd stay downstairs so he couldn't creep out; she'd force him to talk. Anyway, what was the point of going to bed when she wouldn't be able to sleep? However, sleep did come – that fitful disturbed sleep that leaves you more exhausted when you wake than you were before you slept.

The creak of the stairs roused her and as she opened her eyes she focused on Geoffrey standing in front of her, shoes in his hand, his expression one of almost pure hatred. As she had suspected, he had attempted to leave without speaking to her, and finding her waiting for him had obviously annoyed him.

'Why, Geoffrey?' she had almost whispered.

'Isn't it obvious?' he snarled. 'You're so arrogant and egocentric. You're so bloody superior and always right, always trying to put me down and make me look small.'

Her jaw dropped incredulously. How could he be so wrong? She loved and idolised him. She fumbled for a response but nothing came, only the sharp prick of tears she so desperately tried to suppress. His angry words had been so sharp and cruel, and so untrue, that she didn't know how to respond. So she sat there, transfixed, while he put on his shoes and grabbed his jacket before bulldozing his way out of the house.

Kate crumpled into her chair and wept.

CHAPTER 3

Those two days were now long gone but four weeks on Kate still felt the same raw desolation and emptiness that she'd felt on the night that Geoffrey had announced his decision to leave. He had not returned and she had not seen him since. He did telephone her once, a few days later, to arrange for a friend to pick up his belongings, but his tone had been short and curt. The coward! He couldn't even say goodbye in person. When Tracey, the twenty-five year-old 'bit of fluff' he worked with, had arrived to collect 'Geoffy's bits and bobs', everything had fallen into place. The long hours at work, the late nights arriving home, the increased number of workshops and courses. Geoffrey had been having an affair. The verbal cruelty, the coldness and the cowardice hadn't stemmed from hatred but from guilt, and Kate had made it so easy for him. By bringing things to a head she had given him an easy exit.

How she had berated herself over these last four weeks for being so blind that she hadn't guessed about his affair and for giving him the opportunity to walk away without having to explain himself. She had been in a constant turmoil for the last month. At times, she could think clearly and knew she was better off without him, but these moments were very rare. Mostly, she was nursing her broken heart and doing her utmost to get through the routine of her daily life without breaking down into tears or showing the world that she was struggling to survive. Her caffeine and nicotine consumption had rocketed while her food intake was virtually zero. She wondered if she would ever feel better, if she would ever feel happy again, if she would ever look forward to another day. At the moment, as she went to bed alone every night, all she wished for was to fall asleep quickly as this was the only time she felt no pain.

As she lay in bed this Saturday morning, Kate pondered the same dilemma that she faced every day she didn't have to work. Was it more painful to stay at home, inside these walls with all their hurtful memories, or was it worse to have to venture out and pretend that everything was fine?

She got up, went downstairs and, two coffees and five cigarettes later, she decided that she had to get out. After her bath she dressed, fixed her hair and her make-up, then grabbing her bag went outside, slamming the front door behind her before any doubts or second thoughts could make her change her mind. The sun beat down on her face as she stood there wondering which way to go, what to do. She concealed her hesitation by searching her bag for her sunglasses and carefully adjusting them onto her nose. She had to decide quickly, had to make a move before the neighbours noticed her acting strangely and came over to check that she was alright, or worse, inquire about Geoffrey. She decided to go into town to buy some new clothes. She had lost so much weight that everything she owned was hanging off her. Also, as Geoffrey had always resented her spending money on herself, her sparse wardrobe really did need replenishing. She didn't feel like driving so she set off for the walk into town.

*   *   *   *   *

Gina woke abruptly at 8am, her body stiff and aching, her legs feeling as if she had run a marathon. She turned to look at Joe who was still sleeping like a baby and wondered how he could look so peaceful after the previous evening. Surely, even in his sleep, he should be showing signs of worry that he may have put the final nail in the coffin? Gina slowly lifted herself out of bed aware that parts of her face, particularly her eyes, were swollen, and she forced herself to look in the mirror. The image that stared back at her was horrifying – a true testament to the battle that had ensued from a totally innocent night out. She shut her eyes trying to block out the reflection and the memories of the confusion, fear and anger that she had endured. Joe stirred, moved his arm to reach out to Gina and, realising that her side of the bed was empty, sat up. His sleepy eyes rested on Gina's face.

'Jesus Christ Gina,' he gasped. 'Did I do that?'

'Oh, so you do remember something then?' she snapped back.

'No, I don't – well, I mean I don't remember doing that.'

Gina sat back down onto the bed still feeling exhausted and looked him straight in the eyes. The cold blue eyes of the previous night were replaced with something soft and gentle. Joe was displaying genuine concern and his whole body crumpled as he buried his face into his hands.

'Gina, I am so sorry. I really don't know what to say to you. I was totally out of my head last night and all I can remember is being angry with you for not being home.'

Gina was in no mood to listen to his excuses and decided that she needed a soothing shower, a cup of coffee and a cigarette before she could even begin to enlighten her husband.

'I'm taking a shower, Joe. We'll talk later,' she said, turning her back on him as she walked into their ensuite bathroom. 'Right now I suggest you get out of bed and go to collect Kieran from mums. I can't let her see me like this.'

'Okay,' he said obediently, pausing before he continued. 'But I do love you.'

Gina almost smiled at the irony.

After Joe had left the house, Gina made-up her face doing the best she could to cover the bruises and the thick lip. She needed to go into town to buy Kieran a new uniform because he was starting school after the summer holidays. This was the perfect excuse to get out of the house for a few hours to get away from Joe. It was also an outing that she knew he would find acceptable. Thankfully, the sun was shining brightly – a welcome contrast from the previous day's weather meaning Gina could cover her eyes with a pair of sunglasses.

On the bus, Gina reflected on her life with Joe and forced herself to confront the bad times she had shared with him. But she also remembered how she had cried when he told her about his childhood and how he had suffered at the hands of his abusive mother and stepfather. Joe would never admit that he needed help to come to terms with the pain and hurt that he had endured for many years. God knows she had tried to convince him that seeking professional help was not a sign of weakness or failure, but he wouldn't listen and so she had decided to give up on the idea entirely. Gina had only glimpsed this dark side of him before they were married and had felt she was the one to give him the love he had always yearned for. And, indeed, in some respects her love had helped him to conquer some of his demons, enabling him to become a wonderful father and quite a good husband – when he was sober. Since Kieran was born, the drinking sessions had been few and far between but they always resulted in a violent show of insecurity and jealousy. Gina was more worried about the fact that the incidents were becoming progressively worse, culminating in last night's incident where, for the first time, she had actually feared for her life. She shuddered as she thought about the knife, which she had managed to hide under the sofa cushion when he had finally flaked out. She knew the time had now come to give him an ultimatum.

Gina arrived in the town centre and set off towards her favourite store armed with enough cash to buy Kieran's uniform and anything she might fancy. One of the good things about Joe was that he was a hard worker and always generous with the housekeeping money. She never had to ask him for anything as she had more than enough to pay for food and clothes and even managed to save a few pounds a week. Most of the clothes she browsed through did not suit her small curvy frame and anyway, she was in no condition to try new clothes and feel pleased with the result. Instead Gina decided to clear her head with a cup of coffee and made her way down the high street. Her thoughts were interrupted by the sound of someone calling her name.

'Gina? Gina! Wait, Gina!' The voice grew louder. Gina stopped, turned to look behind her and smiled warmly as her gaze rested upon a familiar face from the past.

'Kate? Kate Hart. Is it really you? Well, I never!' she exclaimed as she made her way towards her old friend.

'Yes – It really is me,' Kate said excitedly as the two women hugged each other with great affection. 'It's so good to see you after all this time! How are you? What have you been up to?'

'I'm fine. A little bit older, but no wiser. You look different Kate, but then it must be at least twelve years since we last saw each other,' she replied as she continued to hold Kate's hand. 'Gosh, I can't believe that it's been that long.'

'You haven't changed one bit Gina – I recognised you immediately. Funnily enough I was thinking about you only the other day when I was tidying up a cupboard and came across an old album full of photos. It was when we were both at college and we went to that fancy dress party.'

'Oh yes, *that* fancy dress party,' Gina replied with a giggle. 'We went as 'Charlie's Angels', you were Farrah Fawcett and I was Jaqueline Smith but I don't think I want to remember the rest!'

'I don't think I can remember the rest,' Kate joked but her smile did not reach her eyes.

There was a moment's pause as the two girls hesitated, not knowing what to say to each other next. Even though they had been such close friends, the many intervening years had left them with so much to say that they didn't know where to begin. Gina took note of the sadness in Kate's liquid blue eyes and the message in her body language. This was not the Kate she had known so many years ago. Gone was the confident and almost arrogant air that had always surrounded her persona. In its stead was a vulnerability that she had seen many times before, but never in Kate.

'I was just going for coffee. Have you got time to join me so that we can catch up on each other's news? I want to know all the juicy bits, please,' Gina commanded, linking her arms tightly around Kates as she manoeuvred her towards her favourite coffee shop.

Kate smiled broadly as she allowed herself to be steered. 'I'd love to,' she replied and then added wistfully, 'God Gina, where have all the years gone? It seems like only yesterday when we were both at college, making plans for our bright and successful futures. I've heard that you're married and have a baby – a boy, isn't it?'

'Yes but he's not a baby anymore. Kieran's five now and absolutely scrummy,' corrected Gina. 'But come on you, let's get some coffee first.'

As they sat down at the table, Gina took off her sunglasses, momentarily forgetting the state of her face, and looked up at Kate. Kate gasped as she reached out to touch Gina's face,

'What the hell have you done to yourself?'

Gina hesitated before replying flippantly. 'Oh, I went swimming and got hit by a wave,' and then seeing Kate's serious expression, quickly added, 'It's nothing, honestly – I'm okay.'

Kate crossed her arms. 'And you, young lady, were always very good at hiding your feelings with facetious remarks but excuse me if I insist you try again. Something resembling the truth would be good,' she chided with a frown.

'Now I can see why you became a teacher and I must say I wouldn't want to be in your class,' Gina teased, but her friend was not smiling. She tried another tactic. 'Okay, so I'm not okay, but I asked you first. So come on. I want to hear everything, please and in detail and then you can tell me why you look so unhappy.'

'Bossy as ever!' remarked Kate as she took two cigarettes out of the pack and handed one to Gina. 'I take it you still do?'

'Yeah, it might be the eighties now but some things never change.' Gina laughed; feeling relieved that she had succeeded in sidetracking her old friend.

Kate went on to explain how, just a month ago, her world had been turned upside down by her common-law husband walking out on her and how she had found out that he had been having an affair with some fluff head behind her back, for God knows how long. Gina noticed how much weight she had lost and how her long, blonde, wavy hair lacked its former glory. Her heart just bled for the woman with whom she had shared her college days. There had been a time when the two women would have known every detail of each other's daily lives but now Gina was feeling guilty that she had not even known about the existence of one 'Geoffrey, bastard of the year'. *At least Joe was faithful – that was something, wasn't it?* she thought to herself.

Gina listened to the whole story intently, not missing a single word, as Kate not only brought her up to date on recent events but also took great dramatic joy in reliving her exploits from the time she went to University to the present day. Both women cried, laughed and sometimes shrieked over their coffee, smoking far too many cigarettes. It was the most therapeutic morning either of them had spent for many months.

Gina looked at her watch and suddenly jumped up. 'I must go home now, Kate. Kieran will be waiting for me and I still have to buy him a new school uniform.'

'Aren't you going to tell me what's been happening to you?' asked Kate, aware that she had done all the talking.

'Sorry, I haven't really got time now, but let's get together for a drink one evening. I really enjoyed this morning and I think we'll both need a good friend over the next few weeks. I'll tell you everything then, I promise.'

'Okay,' Kate agreed. 'But just answer me one question. Does he hit you often Gina and do you intend to stay with him?'

'That's two questions Kate,' Gina mocked gently as she tried to remain vague, 'but the answer is yes.'

Kate looked concerned but unimpressed. 'Well, next time we meet perhaps you can explain why an intelligent woman, such as yourself, keeps getting into the ring for another round.' Her deliberate tone reflected her determination to get the truth. Kate proceeded to write her phone number and address on a piece of paper and handed it to Gina. Anxious to lighten the mood she added, 'Oh, and by the way, I must warn you – I haven't had a drink for five years!'

'How many?' Gina looked astonished. 'Are you telling me that no alcohol has passed your lips for five years?'

'That's right,' laughed Kate, as she took Gina's telephone number and put it in her handbag. 'Zilch, nada, zero!'

Gina held an expression of disbelief. 'For Goodness sake, where did that Geoffrey keep you – in the cellar, wearing a nun's outfit? This is definitely not the Kate I know and love. We're going to have to rectify this outrage, as soon as possible. So, I suggest you go and buy yourself a pretty frock or two and I'll give you a call soon.'

The friends left the café, kissed each other goodbye and walked off in opposite directions, both with a hopeful smile and a spring in their steps.

CHAPTER 4

Gina couldn't wait to see Kieran. Although they had only been apart for one night, she had missed him. As she reached the front door she could hear his giggly voice and, once inside, Gina could see a very messy kitchen where father and son had been busy cooking.

As soon as Kieran saw his mother he ran to greet her with his arms outstretched. Gina dropped her shopping bags in the hallway to embrace him.

'Mummy, mummy. Me and daddy have made a chocolate cake for you. Come and see, mummy,' he shouted as he grabbed her hand and pulled her into the kitchen. 'We haven't eaten any yet 'cos we've been waiting for you, haven't we daddy?' Kieran looked up at Joe, who was smiling nervously and searching Gina's face for some clue. Gina did not look at Joe but instead feigned admiration for the unidentifiable, round, brown blob that was splattered onto her kitchen table.

'That looks lovely Kieran,' she smiled. 'What did I do to deserve such a treat?'

'Daddy said that you hurt yourself in an accident - poor mummy. So this is to make you feel better. Shall we have some cake now?' he asked, as he poked his finger through the chocolate topping.

Joe ruffled Kieran's hair. 'In a minute, Kieran. Let me make mummy a nice cup of tea first while you clean yourself up and change your clothes. Then we'll all have some cake. Okay?'

Pleased with himself, Kieran nodded then ran up the stairs and into the bathroom.

Gina started to clear up the mess, all the time avoiding Joe's little boy lost look, and waited for him to make a remark. It eventually came.

'You were shopping a long time,' he said. Yet another one of his statements that was more questioning than mere observation. Gina turned to face him, leaning against the kitchen sink.

'Yes, I bumped into an old college friend. Do you remember me telling you about Kate?' He shook his head, not really sure if she was telling him the truth. She ignored the look on his face and continued.

'Well, anyway, we haven't seen each other for years so we went for a coffee and had a good old natter.' She paused and then with a slight edge to her voice, added sarcastically. 'Alright with you?'

She turned back towards the sink and continued washing up.

'Of course it's alright with me and I'm glad you had a good time,' Joe replied as he moved to sit at the table not daring to look her in the eye.

An uncomfortable silence prevailed for a few seconds.

'Okay Joe, I'm ready to talk about last night now.' Gina wiped her hands, sat down at the kitchen table and looked Joe straight in the eyes. 'You could have killed me,' she said putting her hand up before Joe could protest. 'And don't say anything, just listen.' He nodded, in agreement. 'If it wasn't for the fact that you dragged me upstairs rather than into the lounge, it could have been a very different story this morning. I was petrified at the sight of that knife and I couldn't sleep until I'd hidden it.'

Joe looked astonished.

'I would never have used it,' his eyes begged for her trust as he implored, 'Gina, listen to me. I can't explain why I did any of it really, or even tell you what I did. It's just a drunken blur to me. I'm so sorry. Please forgive me.' He moved towards her to put his arms around her but she stood up to avoid contact.

'Joe, I'm not sure I'm ready to forgive you just yet, but for Kieran's sake I'm going to give you one last chance. Believe me when I say that this is the last time I'll allow you to hurt and humiliate me this way, so if you *ever* lay a finger on me again, that'll be it, I swear. I'll take Kieran and I'll walk out of this marriage for good. No discussion and no more chances. And if you can't control yourself when you're drinking then I suggest that you just don't drink. Do you understand, Joe?' Her big brown eyes were flashing with determination and Joe was left with no doubt that she truly meant it.

Joe sighed with relief. 'I promise it'll never happen again. I love you and Kieran more than anything and I *will* make you both happy.' He moved towards her and this time managed to secure a quick hug, but then Gina gently pushed him away.

'I haven't finished yet, there's something else I want to say. I've decided to go back to work when Kieran starts school. Only part-time to start with, but its something I need to do. I know that you've said no to this in the past but it's different now that Kieran no longer needs me every hour of the day.'

'But we don't need the money,' Joe said looking baffled.

'It's not about the money and you know it. I need to be me again and not just a wife or a mother, and I can't stay at home all day on my own – it'll drive me insane and, besides, the extra money will be useful. I think you'd be quite happy to keep me at home every day under lock and key, given half a chance.'

'That's not true. I want you to be happy.'

'Do you? Well in that case, prove it by giving me your blessing.'

Joe paused, 'Okay. If that's what you really want. Go ahead.'

'Great, thanks.' Gina took a deep breath and, determined to be true to the agreement she had previously formulated in her mind, asserted. 'And there's one last thing. I would like to go out with my friends at least once a month, to the pictures, for a drink, whatever, and for you to accept this without sulking or setting unreasonable restrictions to my evening.'

'Why do you suddenly want to start going out? Haven't you got everything you need, right here in this house?' Joe stood up and reached for the kettle.

'Yes, of course I have, but that's not the point. It's not normal to revolve your whole life around only family. We all need friends. You have them, so sorry, but you're going to have to trust me and accept that I need other people in my life too. If you're not able to do that, then we have no long-term future together.'

This was suddenly all a bit too much for Joe and he knew Gina was probably taking full advantage of his guilty feelings, but he also knew that it was not an unreasonable request. Besides, starting work would give her the new interests that she needed, so hopefully there was a real chance that she wouldn't persevere with this particular goal.

'Okay,' he finally conceded.

'Good,' said Gina, glad that this particular conversation was over with. 'Now let's eat cake!'

At that moment, the phone rang.

CHAPTER 5

Kate paid the taxi driver, collected her packages and walked to her front door. As she turned the key in the lock she realised that, for the first time that she could remember, her heart didn't sink to the pit of her stomach at the prospect of entering her home. She'd called it 'her home' and it hadn't felt like home for so long, but now it did. Good old Gina, her dear, sweet friend. How concerned about her Gina had been, and how she had succeeded in lifting Kate's spirits, despite the fact that she had her own troubles. Kate hadn't felt so good in a long time and it was all due to Gina's unique medicine. Now that they had met up again, Kate was determined not to let their friendship lapse any more, not only for the selfish reason of her needing her friend, but also because she knew that Gina would be needing her and judging by her face, probably quite soon.

Once inside, the impeccably tidy Kate went immediately upstairs and hung her purchases on the wardrobe doors. When she had parted from Gina she started shopping with a vengeance. She had exorcised the ghosts of Geoffrey's meanness and by the time she had finished, her plastic was positively steaming. She had bought new work clothes, new casual attire and, as Gina had instructed, several evening outfits. Money was not an issue for Kate; she earned a good salary and as she hadn't spent much on herself over recent years, she had accumulated some substantial savings that she'd deposited into a building society account, unbeknown to Geoffrey. She had thoroughly enjoyed putting a sizeable dent in it earlier today. Having finished shopping she decided to get a taxi home as she couldn't wait to try them on again at her leisure.

She went back down to the kitchen to make herself a cup of coffee. As she waited for the kettle to boil she looked around the ground floor of her small, two-bedroomed, terraced town house. It suddenly didn't look empty anymore but just neat and tidy as it always used to. In fact, she noticed that her distinctive red and cream lounge looked more luxurious without the presence of Geoffrey's tasteless clutter and even the clean squares on the walls were preferable to his pathetic, amateurish attempts at oil painting. The kettle clicked off and, as she made her coffee, Kate felt sufficiently celebratory to add a teaspoon of Tia Maria. Gina was right; her abstinence had been criminal, but she had better not overdo it; she must get used to alcohol again slowly.

Kate took her coffee upstairs to sip while she tried on her new clothes. What should it be first? The purple Jacques Vert suit or the Principles slinky black-beaded dress? The floaty Monsoon skirt or the skin-tight leather trousers? She had so much to choose from. Kate chose the purple Jacques Vert. Its soft tailoring was so very elegant yet very smart – if only she had a wedding to go to. *Well, it certainly won't be my own*, she thought, feeling pleased that she was at last able to make light of her situation. She smiled at herself in the mirror. She had chosen well, the outfit looked good on her and she looked good in it, thanks to her recent weight loss. It's true what they say, every cloud does have a silver lining and this was the easiest stone she'd ever lost. As she tried on the other purchases her spirits lifted even more, as every outfit looked better on her than the last. By the time she had tried on everything she was bursting to tell someone, and that someone had to be Gina. She extracted the number from her handbag and dialled it on the upstairs extension.

'Hi Gina, it's me, Kate, Are you alright to talk?'

'Of course.'

'I just had to tell you, I've taken your advice and bought myself about half a dozen party outfits. That should see me through until about Christmas!'

The two women continued their light-hearted banter until Kate interrupted:

'Sorry Gina, there's someone at the door.'

'Shall I hold on while you see who it is?' replied Gina.

'No, it's Okay. I'll look out of the window.' She picked up the phone cradle and walked across the bedroom. 'Oh shit! It's him. What does he want?' Kate's voice rose as she tried to suppress her shock.

'What does *who* want? Who are we talking about?' Gina asked.

'There's only one 'Him' – Geoffrey, of course!' Kate screeched in panic.

'Okay, Kate! Now calm down. Find out what he wants.'

Kate popped her head out of the bedroom window and mustering all her composure looked down and called out. 'I'm up here Geoffrey, what do you want?'

Geoffrey looked up and gave a friendly wave. 'Oh, hi Kate! Sorry to bother you but I can't find my passport and realised that I must have left it here.'

'Hang on a minute, I'm on the phone. I'll come down as soon as I can,' she replied trying not to appear flustered but, as she retreated into her bedroom, she tripped over the phone lead. Gina heard her muttering a few expletives before she picked up the receiver and breathlessly responded.

'Sorry Gina, I tripped up and dropped the phone. The bastard wants his passport and I bet he's planning to take that floozie away. Oh my God, I'm not dressed! I'd better go. I'll call you back…'

'Okay! Okay! Now take a couple of deep breaths and calm down Kate. Get yourself dressed and as soon as you've got rid of him you call me back immediately, do you hear me?'

'Yes! Yes! Okay Gina. Bye.' Kate slammed the receiver back into its cradle and stood motionless, her mind in utter turmoil as she thought about Geoffrey on the doorstep waiting to come in. *Does he really want his passport or is it an excuse? Does he really want to come back to me? Is it all over with the floozie? Do I want him back? Of course you do. You stupid cow!* Her mind raced and then at that precise moment Kate glanced at her new clothes and decided what she would do – she would make him realise what he'd given up. She glanced in the mirror and thanked God she'd made herself up to go out today. Her make-up was still intact and her golden waves cascaded around her pretty face. She snatched the Principles black, slinky dress from its hanger and slipped it on.

'Oh no! My bra-straps show and it's over the top,' she almost squealed in her panic. She exchanged the dress for the skin-tight leather trousers – much more appropriate. She rummaged through her sweaters and tops and, in a very un-Kate like manner, flung them far and wide until she found the perfect partner for the trousers – a tight cerise sleeveless silk sweater that hugged every contour of her curvaceous body. She slipped it on and one last glance in the mirror confirmed that she looked good. She inhaled deeply, stuffed the mess she'd made out of sight under her bed, glided downstairs and opened the front door.

'Sorry to keep you waiting for so long but the phone call took longer than I expected,' she said serenely. Kate smiled inwardly as a look of complete desire took hold of Geoffrey's face. Kate knew he found her attractive – that was one part of their relationship that had never been in doubt. Her recent weight loss and the glow she had today only enhanced her looks. *Ah-ha*, she thought, *the desired effect.*

'How rude of me Geoffrey, do come in,' Kate added as she savoured the moment, pleased with herself at the way she was handling the situation.

'About your passport, I can't recall seeing it recently. It's certainly not with my official documentation as I've had to go through that recently, for obvious reasons, and as you know, I would have remembered coming across something like that.' Kate lied with surprising ease.

She could see Geoffrey didn't believe her, as he knew she was meticulously tidy and well organised. Geoffrey told her not to worry about the passport in a dismissive way and then started to compliment her on how the house looked, and more importantly, how she looked. He asked for a coffee, if it was not too much trouble, and continued with his seduction. By the time he was telling her that he had made the biggest mistake of his life, Kate believed her plan had worked.

He scooped her into his arms, carried her upstairs and laid her gently onto the bed. He began to kiss her gently, first on her face and then on her neck and as he undressed her, he kissed every part of her he exposed. She succumbed completely to his attention and responded with equal ardour. He made love to her in the most gentle and passionate way – the way he used to in their early days together and Kate felt complete again. As they lay together afterwards talking gently Geoffrey nonchalantly remarked, 'You do know where my passport is, don't you?'

Kate smiled mischievously. 'Of course I do, and you knew all along I did. I don't mislay things like that. It's in the top drawer of my bureau.'

'Well thanks for that,' he smirked, as he stood up and looked down over her. 'Now I'd better get dressed and be out of here.'

Kate looked horrified and stunned as she watched him hastily gather up his clothes.

He turned to face her as he dressed. 'Oh! Come on Kate, you didn't really think that meant anything, did you? You wanted to play games so I just joined in. I need my passport. Tracey and I are getting married in the

Caribbean next month. Think of this as your wedding present to me,' he sneered.

'You bastard! I always knew you had a nasty streak but I just didn't realise how evil you could be. Get out of my house, now! I never want to see you again.'

She stopped abruptly. Tears were welling up in her eyes and there was no way this excuse for a man was going to see that he'd hurt her again. Geoffrey finished dressing and went downstairs. She heard the bureau drawer open and the front door slam shut.

Kate let her tears escape, but the torrent she expected didn't come. She had already cried enough over him and there was nothing left inside her. The hurt was still there and she was raw inside. However, it wasn't that "I don't know what to do with myself ache" but that "I can't be bothered to do anything" numbness.

Kate couldn't recall how long she'd been sitting on her bed when the phone rang. It was Gina.

'Kate, what's been happening? You promised you'd phone me back. I've been listening out for the phone for ages.'

'I'm so sorry Gina,' she said and then went on to explain the whole sordid episode.

Gina listened intently, offering words of comfort and support, and when she finally managed to extract a small half chuckle from Kate she arranged for them to meet up the following Friday for a night out.

Kate hesitated and then said, 'Gina, I hope you don't mind, but what with the school holidays, I can't face a week at home with nothing to do everyday. I'm thinking of going to visit Sandie and David in Surrey for a few days, but I'll be back by Friday.'

'Of course I don't mind, why should I? I think it's a great idea. It'll do you good to get away for a few days and I'll see you next week. Take care and have a good time.'

'And you take care of yourself too. Thanks Gina, you're one in a million. Bye.'

*   *   *   *   *

Kate drove herself to Surrey the next day. She'd let her parents know her plans but hadn't given them a detailed explanation, as they would only worry and that would be of no use to anyone. They liked Sandie and David and knew they would look after their heartbroken daughter. They were right. Kate was fussed over from the moment she arrived. Sandie had been Kate's best friend at university and they had a natural empathy for one another even though they were quite different. Sandie, who had been a stereotypical laid-back hippie student with her glossy black hair worn long and straight, had matured into a giving and caring earth mother with a heart of gold. She had never had any real ambition beyond becoming a mother and had, in fact, only gone to university so as not to be parted from David. David was Sandie's childhood sweetheart and they were all together at training to become teachers. He was a decent man, solid and reliable but not boring and this was reflected in his open face and kind brown eyes. In their final year they had got married, with Kate as chief bridesmaid. Soon after, Oliver was born, shortly followed by Kirsty. David, who had always been devoted to Sandie, had proved to be an excellent husband and father who revelled in both roles. He was also a most ingenious provider who could make money go further than anyone else Kate knew, just so he could indulge his wife and children. He had joined the Royal Army Education Corps and was currently in barracks in Surrey, which had proved so fortuitous for Kate. Although they had always kept in regular contact, he had been stationed abroad in recent years and it had been almost impossible for them to see each other. Their four-year assignment in Surrey would be different.

In the few days they spent together, it felt like they had never been apart. There was a natural ease between them all, and her friend's cosseting and advice had been very therapeutic for her. By the time Kate left she was feeling much happier and stronger and vowed to become a regular houseguest. She was surprised by how positive she felt on the drive home and was really looking forward to seeing Gina the following evening – and to tidying up the mess from under her bed!

When Kate walked through her front door she was stunned by the most wonderful surprise. Her dear, sweet parents had redecorated her lounge, in the same colour she'd always had, as they wouldn't be so presumptuous as to alter it. However the fresh paint had eliminated all traces of Geoffrey. They had also left fresh flowers in a vase on the windowsill, some basic food supplies in the fridge and a box of Belgian chocolates on the coffee table. Kate looked around admiringly at her neat and perfect home, decorated in such excellent taste and immaculately tidy, just as it was before she had ever met Geoffrey. It suddenly dawned on her that he was not quite as evil as she had once thought. He could have been really nasty and demanded half of her home. As her common-law husband, the law of the land would have been on his side. But he didn't, he just took his belongings along with his car. Was it out of well-hidden decency, or just plain guilt? Anyway, why care? It was all over between them now. She was better off without him and one day she would truly believe that.

Kate sat in her favourite armchair, still admiring her parent's hard labour. She was so lucky, she had her beautiful home, her wonderful parents who never interfered but were always there for her, her dear friends Sandie and David who had always been so kind. And of course, she had Gina, who had once been her closest friend but when Kate had gone off to university they had lost touch. How she had missed her over the years, but now fate had brought them together again and it was as though they had never been apart. They were bound to have some more great times together and with that thought Kate lifted the phone to call Gina, to confirm the first of these tomorrow night.

CHAPTER 6

As Kate stirred from her deep slumber she groaned loudly. It was not a groan for effect – indeed she was alone and there was no one around to be affected by it. No, she groaned because of the excruciating pain in her head. It was more than the proverbial "axe through the head" type headache, it was more like a magician's sword trick that had failed and pierced her skull with numerous sharp blades. Her mouth felt like the entire contents of a cat's litter tray and her breath was undoubtedly just as sweet. As she moved slightly she felt strangely uncomfortable and then the awful realisation of her current state hit her. She was in her own bed covered neatly with her duvet, but she was fully dressed, complete with her coat, shoes and even her handbag over her shoulder.

Oh, my God, she thought as she slowly began to remember the events of the previous night – her long awaited night out with Gina. But the after-effects of the demon drink took hold of her fragile skull again and she concentrated her attentions on her immediate predicament. She slowly got up, each movement sending another searing pain through her brain, which, at this moment, felt like something akin to scrambled eggs. Slowly, she discarded all her clothes including her shoes, coat and bag before putting on her bathrobe and descending the stairs one tentative step at a time. After a much-needed fix of caffeine, nicotine and aspirin she ran a hot, deep bubble bath and as she luxuriated in the tub she began to recall the evening's events.

It had all started so well. Kate had taken her time to get ready, her make-up and hair had gone well and when she slipped on the Principles slinky black beaded dress and some black high-heeled sandals the transformation was complete. Kate had never been one for false modesty and she knew she looked good. When the pre-booked taxi arrived she grabbed her coat and bag and headed off for the wine bar at which they had arranged to meet. When she arrived Gina was waiting for her, looking equally stunning in a red dress which was just the right shade to bring out the highlights of her titian hair without clashing. Two glasses of chilled white wine were already on the table. The friends chatted, catching up on each other's news and laughing at how good they both looked and how the town was in for a shock now that they were back in circulation. Gina ordered a second glass of wine but, being out of practice, Kate was still on her first. They spent a happy couple of hours in the wine bar chatting to each other and to friends that came in, although these were mainly Gina's friends as Kate had been out of the picture for so long that she knew hardly anybody outside of her own work circle.

At around eleven they moved on to a nightclub that was new to both and once inside, Kate ordered the drinks. Feeling happy, she ordered herself a gin and tonic, her tipple of years gone by. This proved to be her big mistake. They danced and chatted, but by the time she was half way through her drink Kate began to feel unwell. She'd had two glasses of wine beforehand but, as she had been too excited to eat, this was enough of a mix, on top of her empty stomach and her years of abstinence, to make her feel really ill. She made her excuses and dashed to the Ladies where she immediately got over-friendly with the white porcelain. She was obviously there a lot longer than she had thought, as a concerned Gina eventually came looking for her. Gina helped Kate clean herself up and got her a glass of water. Although concerned for her friend she couldn't help finding the situation amusing – what a state to get into after a mere two glasses of wine and a G&T. Even Kate saw the funny side of it all. Gina took her to sit in the quieter reception area and even managed to sweet-talk a barman into making Kate a coffee.

Kate winced with embarrassment as she remembered the scene. How was she ever going to face that nightclub again? The coffee had had little effect and so Gina decided to take Kate home by taxi. Gina wanted to come in with Kate but Kate insisted she go on home. She knew the consequences would be dire if she didn't get home to Joe and she knew that if Gina didn't keep this taxi it would be ages before she could get another one. Once at her house Gina alighted with Kate to make sure she was okay. Kate had to almost insist she got back into the taxi but only after Gina insisted she heard her lock herself in.

'I'm shutting the door now, I'm putting the bolt across now, I'm putting the chain across now, I'm safely locked in Gina. Thank-you, I love you, take care, see you soon, love you lots, I'll phone, bye,' Kate rambled.

Gina said her goodbyes through the door and left.

She must have mustered all the remnants of her *compos mentis* to get indoors safely because she could not remember a single moment from saying goodbye to Gina until that painful meeting with consciousness this morning.

Kate's bath had made her feel better, if still a little fragile. Once dressed and after more coffee and a painful slice of toast – her stomach was still tender after last night's retching – she pondered phoning Gina, but hesitated. She had a feeling it might aggravate Joe if Gina got a call from a friend today. She knew Gina would be thinking of her and would phone her to check that she was okay if she got the chance. So instead, she busied herself by clearing up the mess she'd made in the wake of last night, namely changing her bed linen and laundering it along with her outfit. A simple task of little consequence normally, but today in her fragile state one that required supreme effort and concentration. It was almost as if she saw this as a penance for her ungainly behaviour last night.

* * * * *

Gina arrived at her front door, seemingly oblivious to the fact that she was more than an hour later than the 1am dictated to her by Joe. Though not drunk – looking after Kate all evening had certainly put paid to that – she was unsteady on her feet and flashbacks of the evening's events had made her giggle to herself as she gently let herself into the house. The memory of the sight of poor Kate after her episode in the ladies made her want to laugh out loud. Kate had arrived at the wine bar with a convincing air of total confidence and looking a million dollars. After an initial nervousness, which saw her smoking cigarettes at the six an-hour mark, she had calmed down and was beginning to relax and enjoy herself. That was the case until a fateful G&T brought her night to a very unladylike end. Kate emerged from the ladies with wild, tangled hair and remnants of eye make up that had formed streaks of black lines across the top of her cheekbones. It was one of the funniest sights Gina had seen in a long time.

The total darkness in Gina's hallway brought her back to the present and she made a conscious effort to be as quiet as possible. What was the time? Was she late? Was Joe asleep and, more importantly, had he been drinking? He had promised her the contrary. To be on the safe side Gina took off her shoes and tiptoed up the stairs towards the bedroom. She had decided against making a cup of tea and smoking a last cigarette in case she woke Joe even though she was gasping for a thirst-quenching hot drink. Something told her it was best to end the night while the going was good. Shoes in her hand, she slowly opened the bedroom door and tried to make out the time on the bedside alarm clock which shone out into the darkness. *Oh my God, two o'clock. How did it get to be that late?*

Without warning the bedroom light jumped into life and Joe sat bolt upright.

'I'm sorry Joe, I didn't mean to wake you,' Gina whispered not wanting to wake Kieran.

'That's okay, but where have you been?' Joe asked sleepily, suppressing his irritation. Gina caught the slight bittersweet smell of whisky and her heart sunk. With the adrenaline that was beginning to pump around her body, Gina sobered up completely and decided to try the "glad to be home, had a boring evening" approach so as not to antagonise him further.

'Yes I know I'm a bit later than we agreed, but you promised not to drink,' she concluded lamely knowing instantly it was the wrong answer.

'Are you taking the piss, Gina? I see, so it's okay for you to go out boozing, showing off your bits to all and sundry, while I stay at home like the mug that you think I am, is it?' Joe was becoming angry, but still in control, and Gina knew that she was not in any danger. She put her arms around him and kissed him hard on the cheek. 'Stop being silly Joe. You know I love you and I don't think you're a mug for one moment. Let's go to sleep and I'll tell you all about tonight in the morning.'

Joe relented, albeit begrudgingly, gave her a kiss goodnight and turned off the light, leaving Gina concerned but too tired to ponder for now.

CHAPTER 7

Gina was excitedly preparing herself for her interview. It was for a small company looking to recruit a part-time bookkeeper for three days a week. Her friend Claire had stumbled across the vacancy and promptly alerted Gina knowing that it was just what she had been looking for. Gina did not have much in the way of suits or office wear, as it had been several years since she had needed such finery, but luckily Claire was the same height and size as Gina and kindly lent her one of her most expensive professional outfits for the occasion. More than anything Claire was excited at the prospect of her dear friend working nearby and it meant that they would sometimes be able to have lunch together.

Unbeknown to Gina, Claire also knew the person who would be carrying out the interview and had put a good word in for her. His name was Richard, an architect and a client of the solicitors where Claire worked. In fact, Claire's desire for Gina to be successful was twofold. Apart from it meaning that she could spend more time with Gina, she was hoping it was also a way of getting closer to Richard on a more personal level. For she had fallen in lust with him at first sight and her instincts told her that the feeling was mutual, but opportunities for anything to develop were non-existent at the office. She had felt guilty for not telling Gina of this little secret, but Claire exonerated herself by deciding that everyone would be a winner – a justified means to an end.

Gina felt fantastic in the beautiful navy suit teamed with a crisp, white blouse and navy accessories. Kieran had been at school for two weeks now and Joe was at work so Gina had enjoyed taking more than two hours to get ready. The result was more than worth it. Gina felt so positive about the whole adventure and knew that her previous experience would be enough to get her the job, but she also knew that personality played a big part. Her planning had allowed for time to receive calls and she had not been disappointed when her mother, Kate and Claire all phoned wishing her luck and telling her to "knock 'em dead". It didn't surprise her in the least that Joe had forgotten to call her, but at least he had given her his blessing when she told him about the interview. In fact she was convinced it was genuine so he was obviously just busy at work and unable to get to the phone. Gina took one last look in the mirror, a deep breath and picked up an umbrella in case it rained and ruined her rigidly fixed-with-spray hair.

The interview was an enjoyable and comfortable experience once she was able to stop herself melting into the big brown eyes of the man sitting opposite her. What a looker! Claire could've at least warned her that he was one of this planet's sexiest creations. However, despite the distraction, at the end of the interview Richard announced that the job was hers and that he would like her to start as soon as possible. Gina managed to contain her excitement until she returned home whereby she promptly returned all the calls of the day in the same order that they had been received. Her mother congratulated her, Kate whooped and Claire screamed, following it up with a confession regarding the man she was going to marry with a little help from her friend. Gina didn't mind one bit and thought that, at that moment, life was just grand.

And for the next three months life was exactly that. Kieran was enjoying school life and took to it without shedding a single tear or exhibiting any concerns about leaving his mother's side. Although a little hurt at his obvious enthusiasm, Gina was thrilled that he had made new friends so easily and was enjoying his new life of education. Gina was also relishing her new-found freedom and her part-time job, which left her with plenty of time to keep the house clean and ensure her boys had a good home-made meal each night. Her days were filled with fun, laughter and new challenges at work and her evenings were filled with contentment and satisfaction with her home life. What Gina hadn't realised, at this joyous time, was that Joe was far from happy. Oh no, he was hiding his total misery caused by her monthly nights out, her lunchtime tête-à-têtes with Claire or Kate and her chatter about all the men in the office, who were so obviously trying to get into her knickers. But then that was Gina – too naïve to see this for herself. He had tried to tell her but she wasn't listening.

One evening as she and Joe were relaxing in front of the television, she told him about Claire and Richard and how close they were becoming.

'Claire would like to know if we fancied a foursome one night,' Gina stated hopefully. 'What do you think?'

Joe continued staring at the screen.

'What do you mean, what do I think? Why would I want to go out with them?' he replied in a lazy voice.

Gina ignored the obvious rejection.

'Well, I thought it would give you a chance to get to know my friends better and…'

'Oh I see. Richard is a friend now, is he? Funny, I thought he was your boss,' he snapped back, giving her a short, sharp glance before he stood up and walked out of the room. As far as Joe was concerned there was nothing more to be said. *Why on earth would he encourage them to be even friendlier than they already were? Sometimes Gina just didn't get it. No, she didn't get it at all.*

*   *   *   *   *

Kate sat staring into the middle distance as she stirred her coffee. She had found herself in the same coffee shop that she and Gina had gone to the day they had bumped into each other, and wondered if her subconscious had brought her here as a good omen, while she pondered her current situation. Her life had settled down since that meeting with Gina and she had found certain contentment with her solitary routine. She was an exceptionally tidy and well-organised individual who revelled in her immaculate home and study. How gratifying it was to be able to keep her home spotless and her paperwork up to date and in order, and not have anyone around to undo all her good work. She also regained her social freedom, which Geoffrey had so long denied her. Being a naturally gregarious, person she enjoyed spending time with others and was often out visiting family and friends. Her parents frequently invited her for a meal, she made several visits to Surrey to stay with David and Sandie and she and Gina were in constant contact, often meeting for lunch and enjoying an occasional night out together. She thoroughly enjoyed teaching, she loved children and often thought how lucky she was to have a career that gave her so much fulfilment.

But, she thought to herself, life always has a 'but' – a niggle that throws a spanner into the works and stops everyone from being totally satisfied with their lot. Her 'but' was Howard, her Head of Department. She had always suspected that he didn't like her and had even confided this feeling to the Deputy Headmistress who had assured Kate that it wasn't that he didn't like her – he just didn't know how to handle her. She was extremely outgoing, gave the impression of being totally confident and on top of all this she was supremely competent. Such a woman was beyond the realms of Howard's experience, and Kate being such a woman posed Howard problems he'd never before encountered. However, the truth came out when he discovered her relationship with Geoffrey was over and he offered his services with anything around the house that she couldn't manage on her own. She had laughed at his smutty innuendo but had inwardly cringed. Howard was a small, weak and bony man with about as much charisma and sex appeal as the average school desk. He had tried to come on to her a few more times and when she had realised that subtlety wasn't going to work Kate had told him bluntly but politely that she was not interested

That was when Kate's trouble began as the mean-spirited Howard turned nasty. Her mother had always warned her to be wary of little men, saying that sometimes what they lacked in trousers they made up for with mouth and, in this case, it was proving to be true. Howard took every opportunity to belittle her in front of colleagues, picking her up for the slightest error and constantly nit-picking to a minuscule degree. She was also sure he was bad mouthing her behind her back. This was putting pressure on Kate and the stress was resulting in her making mistakes that she normally would never have made. Kate was beginning to worry that this might have an adverse effect on her future prospects, or worse, that Howard might actively be trying to destroy them right now.

So here she sat, drinking a solitary cup of coffee and wondering what she should do. She could try to ignore him and hope that he would eventually get bored and stop this vendetta, but this was unlikely; he was a little man who would bear a grudge for a long time. She could sleep with him and get it over and done with, but even thinking of this made her choke and splutter into her coffee cup. She could report him for sexual harassment, but this could backfire as it was only her word against his and with him being her boss and having friends in higher places it would be easier to dispose of Kate. She could well be labelled a troublemaker and this would have far-reaching implications for her career. She could look for another job at a different school, but this would be very difficult thanks to the government and their current cuts in education spending. She could have an unofficial, "off the record" chat with her Deputy Head. Kate had always admired Joyce who was extremely professional and impartial and she knew that she liked Kate. She would just seek her advice on how to handle an awkward situation and at the same time she would be letting her know that it existed. This was it, the obvious first step. Why hadn't she thought of it before? This is what she would do. With that, Kate gathered her belongings and left for a spot of retail therapy.

CHAPTER 8

A car pulled up outside the house and Gina rushed to the window hoping it was a taxi bringing Joe home. He had gone out leaving a note on the kitchen table stating quite curtly that he needed time to think so was going for a couple of drinks with a friend. It was now 9pm and Gina was becoming agitated and worried about where he might be on this freezing Saturday evening. She had tried a couple of his regular haunts and, much to her embarrassment, had seen some of his friends along the way who thought it highly amusing that "her indoors" was hunting down Joe. Little did they realise that this was no laughing matter and that her purpose was to find him before he became so drunk that it would be a serious threat to her well-being.

The day had started really well. They had gone into town and bought Kieran some of his Christmas presents, taken them home to hide and then collected Kieran from her parents. After lunch, Joe promised to complete several unfinished DIY chores and so Gina took the opportunity to take herself and Kieran to visit Kate for a cup of coffee and to discuss how Kate was going to tackle her obnoxious boss. Gina loved to be needed and was at her best when giving advice, although this was quite a tricky situation and one that Gina was glad not to be experiencing. Having analysed every avenue they decided that the most tried and trusted course of action was best after all. Kate would kick Howard in his golden balls as hard as she could and take the consequences. It was also decided that this momentous event would take place when Kate's oestrogen level was at its lowest, thereby ensuring optimum use of aggression. They had laughed so loudly that Kieran ran in from the garden to find out what all the commotion was about.

It was when they had returned home from Kate's that Gina had found the house empty and the note on the table. Gina knew instinctively that she had to take her precious son back to her mother's, and that this time she would not be able to totally conceal from her parents her reason for doing so. After a fruitless search of the pubs he was known to frequent, Gina returned and sunk despairingly into her sofa trying not to cry. It wasn't that she hadn't suspected that he was unhappy with the new Gina, but more that she had made such an effort to ensure that he benefited from her new happiness and had taken time out to give him all the attention and affection any man could possibly want. Well, it obviously wasn't enough for Joe, because he was making a big, self-indulgent point, but Gina's new life was non-negotiable and she had no intention of giving up any of it. Her requests had not been unreasonable and the only person not happy was Joe. She decided to just sit tight and tough it out.

Gina eventually fell asleep on the sofa and woke with a start when she heard Joe slamming the front door. Her eyes felt heavy and her neck ached from the uncomfortable stance she had rested in.

'Is that you Joe?' she called out cheerfully, rubbing her neck and trying to remember why she wasn't in bed.

'Who else would it fucking be?' he spat out at her as he crashed into the doorframe and swayed into the room. 'One of your lovers, eh? Did you think it was one of your lover-boys from work?' he continued, lurching towards her. 'Did you?' he screamed, working himself up into a frenzy.

Gina was wide-awake now as Joe continued to stagger towards her with alarming speed and determination, falling onto his knees in front of her. He persisted with his verbal assault. 'It might as well be, because you don't want *me* anymore, do you? No, I'm not good enough for Miss High and Mighty.

Think you're something special don't you?' he mocked. 'Well, you're fucking not.'

Gina was totally unsure of what to say or how to react, but knew she needed to move away from his reach. She took a deep breath as she rose, but as she took her first step he grabbed her by the legs and pulled her down roughly to the floor, dragging her along until she could feel her flesh burning against the carpet. She tried to pull herself into a kneeling position so that she could attempt a getaway through the back door but he continued to use brute force to keep her in a vulnerable position. No matter how hard she wriggled or lashed out she was no match for his strength and fortitude so, finally exhausted, both physically and mentally, she turned her body to face him. He didn't see her now, so blind was his fury, and she knew there was no point in pleading or screaming. The biggest beating of her life was written in those empty ice blue eyes and she knew that any attempts to avoid it were futile. Her brain raced trying to think of damage limitation tactics, but it was no use and she knew it. Strangely enough, once she gave up on the idea of trying to find a way out, it was almost a relief and the fear she had felt was replaced with a numbness that blocked out the mental anguish she felt by her husband's totally indefensible behaviour. The physical pain was real, but she neither screamed nor cried as he almost beat the breath out of her, punching and kicking her tiny frame until his anger had been sated. He towered over her, sneering triumphantly before staggering up to bed, leaving her motionless and curled up in a little ball. When his footsteps finally faded away she allowed herself to sob as she finally admitted to herself that she had no choice but to leave him.

Gina lay silently for a few minutes before tentatively lifting herself into a sitting position. He'd been clever this time and had avoided hitting her face.

Her hands were throbbing now, having used them to shield the vulnerable parts of her body, but it had been worth it. Although broken spiritually, she convinced herself that her injuries did not warrant a visit to the hospital and this proved to Gina that, even in his fury, he must have been keeping something back. She was sure that if he had used his full power, she would not be conscious now. If that was the case and he was able to control himself to some degree then why could he not restrain himself in the first place? Gina knew what she had to do and there was no time like the present.

She quietly made her way up the stairs and waited at the top until she could hear his drunken snores. Safe in the knowledge that he would not wake easily, she tip-toed her way slowly into the spare bedroom and searched in the darkness for some sort of bag in which to throw a few essentials in. Grabbing her toothbrush and a few clean clothes from the airing cupboard, she made her way back down the stairs. At one point she froze as Joe snorted loudly and she could hear him move about in their bed. Her heart was thumping so loudly it sounded to her like an army of men marching to her rescue.

She reached the bottom of the stairs and threw on the first pair of shoes she could find. After grabbing her coat and handbag, she went to the front door and paused, turning her head to listen out for any movement upstairs. The silence calmed her and with a heavy heart, she gently let herself out.

Once outside, the cold air hit her battered body and momentarily took her breath away. She didn't stop to put on her coat, but just ran as far as her bruised legs would carry her until she reached a telephone box. Rushing inside, she dialled quickly.

'Kate my darling, I need you right now.'

CHAPTER 9

Kate had wasted no time in speaking to Joyce and had explained her situation in the matter-of-fact and impartial manner that she knew Joyce would relate to. Joyce had listened attentively and, after a short silence while she pondered the situation, she had advised Kate to maintain a professional aloofness and as much distance as possible, but also to keep a detailed log of all incidents, just in case. Kate had felt much more confident and calm after this discussion with Joyce, although it had done nothing to alleviate her problem. Howard had continued his attempts to make her working life as miserable as possible; by omitting to inform her of important staff meetings; not passing on parents letters and giving her report cards to complete within unreasonable time limits. However, although his attempts to sabotage her were unbearable at times, Kate had merely recorded each incident in detail in the school exercise book she kept for this purpose, and then got on with her teaching.

Gina moving in, just before Christmas, had also helped a great deal, as it was extremely comforting to have someone to sound off to in the evenings, rather than to sit alone and brood.

The two friends had returned to the bosom of their respective families, for the Christmas festivities, as both had mothers who insisted on nurturing their daughters. Kate's Christmas had been a quiet over-indulgent affair. With no children in the family to entertain it had been one long round of eating, drinking and lazing around watching television. Kate loved being cosseted by her family and it was the one time of the year when she didn't feel guilty about doing nothing except recharging her batteries. However, such a season also emphasises being alone and as Kate grew increasingly aware of the lack of a man in her life, a distinct melancholy set in.

Gina's Christmas had also produced it's own share of angst. Although she too had enjoyed the pleasure of a loving family gathering, it had highlighted the fact that she had dissolved her own family unit. It had been difficult for her to share Kieran with Joe and she had been acutely aware of his absence when he was spending time with his father.

Both women returned to Kate's house just before the New Year and welcomed their reunion. For Gina it was a relief not to have to put on a brave face and for Kate it was good not to have to return to an empty home.

In fact, Gina moving in had been good for her in other ways also. It was a snug fit, the three of them in her small, two-bedroomed Victorian terraced home, with Gina sharing the master bedroom with Kate and Kieran in the spare room. They had decided to give Kieran the spare room to himself, reasoning that this would hopefully minimise the disruption to his young life as he had always been used to his own room. Also, Gina had always been firm about Kieran's set bedtime as he needed his sleep for school. Kate had readily agreed he needed undisturbed sleep, as parents who did not insist on appropriate bedtimes and, as a consequence, sent their children to school too tired to learn properly had always particularly vexed her. The room also doubled as his playroom so he could leave his toys out without them getting in the way at other times. They all got on well together and had developed a good routine without any of the frictions that both women had secretly feared might occur. Even Gina's more *laissez-faire* attitude towards housework and her liberal definition of tidy didn't upset the fastidious Kate and, in fact, evidence of Kieran's playing and her tripping over the odd toy car only made Kate smile at the thought of the dear little chap. It was this that proved to be the great-unexpected benefit for Kate. Being as meticulous as she was and leading a solitary life, Kate was in danger of becoming an obsessive, particularly as she used cleaning and tidying as therapy to help blot out any misery she might be experiencing. It was this tendency that was so effortlessly curbed by the arrival of her two houseguests. A more predictable benefit, with Joe having his son to stay every weekend, was that the two friends were able to go out together far more frequently. It was Gina's turn to revel in her new found freedom and she encouraged Kate to go out as much as possible, not that Kate needed much encouragement as she was also still comparatively new to regular partying. The two friends hit the wine bars and nightclubs with a vengeance and became regular and well-known faces at a few of the better class establishments.

It was on one of these nights out that Kate glanced across the bar and immediately began to sink into the pools of melting chocolate that were the beautiful dark Mediterranean eyes belonging to Mikos. Although he was taller than Kate, he was not overly tall. He was slim and dark and very handsome in a continental sort of way. He walked over to Kate and started chatting to her and she flirted shyly with him, turning her head down and gazing upward and sideways at him through her long eyelashes. She couldn't recall a thing he was saying to her, she was simply lost in his deep voice with its thick accent that made her feel like she was being wrapped in dark velvet. As the end of the evening drew closer, Mikos asked Kate out to dinner the following week and she accepted. Kate floated home recounting every moment to an indulgent Gina who smiled inwardly at her lovesick friend and was so pleased to see that Kate had finally left Geoffrey behind her and was ready to move on in her life.

As the dinner engagement approached Kate was almost bursting with excitement. Gina found it hilarious watching Kate get ready and pondering indecisively about everything, from which outfit to wear to which bath-oil to soak in. Her manic flitting between bathroom and bedroom with diversions to the lounge to ask Gina's opinion on something left Gina in a state of exasperated amusement, but she was the first to admit that all Kate's efforts had been worth it. She looked stunning.

Mikos arrived promptly and as Kate opened her front door to him he expelled a 'Wow!' with a lung-full of air.

He took her to an exquisite little waterfront bistro. As the waiter showed them to their table he whispered to her so closely that he almost caressed her ear with his breath. 'I'm sorry I booked a table at such a modest little restaurant. If I'd realised I was going to escort such a beautiful woman to dinner I would have booked the Ritz.' Kate giggled at the compliment.

Once they were seated he took her hand in his and stroked it tenderly. 'How come such a beautiful princess as you isn't already taken?' he asked as he looked deep into her eyes.

'It's a long story,' Kate replied gently withdrawing her hand, 'but let's just say that after kissing the last prince he turned back into a frog. Well, more a toad really.'

They both laughed and continued their banter.

'Tell me all about yourself,' he pleaded, 'I want to know all about the angel I'm looking at.'

Kate told him about herself, a sanitised version of her less than successful private life and a brief résumé of her professional path. His interest seemed to grow the more he found out about her; he liked her for being a financially independent career woman and admired her success, while mocking the men who had failed to appreciate her. *At last*, Kate thought to herself, *someone who appreciates me for what I've achieved rather than resenting it.* He, in turn, told Kate how he had ended up single and in town. He had moved over here when he married a local girl and despite being an engineer he had to work as a mechanic as his Greek qualifications were not recognised by British firms. His marriage had unfortunately not survived the test of time, but by the time it had ended he'd established a network of friends and felt that home was here, and so had stayed. His marriage had been over for some time but there was no animosity between them and his ex-wife had remarried and started a family.

'But enough of the gloomy past,' he ended. 'I want to enjoy the present, this beautiful evening and the even more beautiful lady I'm sharing it with.'

Mikos continued to be an attentive and charming companion throughout and at the end of the evening escorted Kate home, behaving like the perfect gentleman. The following day an extravagant bouquet of roses was delivered to Kate. The card thanked her for a delightful evening and suggested a trip to the theatre.

And so Kate's new romance began. Mikos courted her slowly, treating her like a lady and behaving like a gentleman. Kate couldn't decide whether he was being quaintly old-fashioned or a traditional *Latino*. It didn't really matter. She just revelled in being treated as someone special. He was an inventive as well as generous consort and their dates varied from dinner, the theatre or cinema to visits to the zoo and a theme park. Always Kate had a marvellous time. Gina was so happy for Kate and grew fond of Mikos, it was obvious he cared for Kate. Sandie and David, however, were protective of their friend and, aware of her still vulnerable emotions, urged caution. Nonetheless they too were delighted to see her so happy and invited her to bring him down to Surrey on her next visit.

Kate's new found happiness was evident to those she worked with also, and many of her colleagues were pleased to see the spark return to their enthusiastic and committed work-mate. Howard however, was not. He stepped up his antagonism towards Kate until she had no choice but to confront him. As she walked into his office, Howard looked up but, without acknowledgement, returned to his writing. After a few moments Kate initiated the conversation without waiting any longer for his permission.

'I need to speak to you, if I may.' Kate paused waiting for a response but when none came continued, 'I feel your treatment of me is unreasonable and I think we need to discuss this, now.'

'Oh, you do, do you Kate?' he replied sardonically but she now had his full attention as he laid his pen down and folded his arms.

'Yes I do. There have been several incidents that have proved to me that you are trying to trip me up and undermine my professionalism. I also feel that you do not give me the support that you give the others and, in fact, sometimes you do the exact opposite,' Kate announced as she sat down and faced him squarely.

'Well there's a very easy solution to this,' he leered at Kate and, seeing her quizzical expression, continued. 'I could be a lot nicer to you, if only you were a lot nicer to me.'

Kate could not believe her ears. 'Are you saying what I think you're saying? Because if you are I must let you know that I have been keeping this.' She slapped the logbook on his desk keeping one finger firmly on it. 'It was Joyce that suggested I keep tabs and your wife will be the first person to receive a copy.'

At this Howard looked flabbergasted, as he had not reckoned on the return of her spirit, and he was left open-mouthed as she picked up the book, turned and walked purposefully out of the room.

So feeling that Howard was now history, life was grand once more. With her friendships solid and her blossoming romance, what more could she ask for? A little more luck and happiness for Gina, perhaps?

*   *   *   *   *

Gina stood on the lawn of the small front garden and looked up at the neat three-bedroomed town house, shielding her face from the spring sunshine with her hand. 'Well, what do you think?' she asked both Kate and Kieran, hopeful of a positive response. Having previously viewed the house alone, she felt that this was the best she could achieve within her budget.

'Well it's not really up to me, is it?' Kate replied turning to Kieran. 'What about you, little man. Do you like it?'

'No, not really,' he mumbled with hands in pockets, hunched shoulders and a grimace. 'My bedroom is too small and I'm too far away from my friends. And if I'm too far away to play with my friends then they won't like me anymore, will they?' He paused and then blurted out, 'And I want daddy to live with us.' His big brown eyes appeared moistened with the first showings of a restrained tear.

'Oh my poor darling,' Gina said bending down to comfort him with a big hug, pulling him close. Kieran's hands remained in his pockets. 'We don't have to move here if you don't want to. Mummy will find somewhere nearer to your friends and close to daddy, I promise.' Standing up she turned to Kate and whispered. 'Oh well that's put paid to that one – again!'

'Look Gina, it's not a problem,' assured Kate genuinely. 'You can stay with me for as long as you like. I love having you both with me and we're having such fun, aren't we?'

Gina's eyes brightened. 'Yes its been great and I really don't know what I would've done without you, but I feel as if you need some space now, what with, you know, Mikos and privacy and all that. It's starting to become awkward.'

Kate could see the strain on Gina's face and decided that instead of their usual Friday night out, they should have a nice evening in, comfort eating, listening to music and chatting. She affectionately put her arm around Gina's shoulder. 'Yes, I know it's a bit difficult sometimes and it would be ideal for Kieran too if you could get him settled again, but let's not rush this. Anyway, we'll get some shopping in for the weekend and then call it a day, shall we? I'll cook us a huge three course meal – fancy that tonight?'

'You must be a mind reader as I was just thinking that I'm really in the mood for being one of the ugly sisters tonight. You know the ones, not doing a lot in sexless clothes and sporting the obligatory horrible hair and pasty face. But if you want to be Cinderella with Mr. Athens then that's alright by me too,' Gina said smiling, knowing that Kate would not change her mind.

'Mr. Athens can wait, and besides you really need two ugly sisters to make it offensive enough to give any real comfort!'

'Well, as long as you're sure, I don't want to spoil your fun just because I'm feeling lazy and a bit...' Ginas voice trailed as she looked at Kieran's crumpled little face. It broke her heart to see him so sad and even though several months had passed since she had left Joe, there were times when she was tempted to go back to him. Not for herself, but for Kieran and for Joe, who were both still begging her to do so. Sometimes the pressure was immense but she knew that Joe would eventually revert to type and for that reason alone she was sure Kieran would benefit more in the long term from their split. However, it was important that both parents showed how much they loved him and didn't argue over every little thing and, at the moment, this was easy because Joe was on his best behaviour in an endeavour to convince Gina that she should return to their marital home. Even when they had first spoken, after she had left him, he had looked resigned and reacted surprisingly well when she told him that she was living with Kate. At first she had not told him the exact location of Kate's house for fear of drunken visits in the middle of the night, and for several weeks Kate had kindly taken Kieran to Joe's each Friday evening. Joe was spending every weekend with his son and the rest of the week working hard while planning new strategies on how to reunite his family. So far it wasn't working but he had optimistically told Gina that he had no intention of giving up just yet. Gina hadn't met anyone else and as long as this was the case, he felt that deep down she still loved him and would give him another chance. Gina had tried to tell him that he should concentrate on moving on with his life, but she was finding it difficult not to appear harsh and uncaring and had, unintentionally, left him with enough hope to cling onto.

That evening, after Gina had kissed her son goodbye for the weekend, she had a long soak in the bath and indulged in the luxurious bubbles for over an hour while Kate prepared the evening meal. Not for the first time did she relive every moment of her last evening with Joe, wondering if she could have done anything differently or given him one last chance. Had she been too hasty in packing her bags, in the middle of the night, while he lay sleeping in a drunken stupor? Should she have stayed for Kieran's sake or was this best for everyone? She couldn't help feeling sorry for him as he spent his week all alone, regretting throwing away his last chance to keep their marriage alive. His pitiful face only added to her feelings of guilt and despair as her mind went round in circles trying to justify Kieran's separation from his father. Only the delicious smell of the food wafting up the stairs encouraged her to leave the warmth and security of the bathroom. For, if the truth had been told, Gina was feeling as much sadness as Kieran and was enjoying the comfort of the water as it disguised her tears and washed away the blues. Gina cried herself to sleep on a regular basis, but while she lay in the bath and analysed everything that had happened she decided that it was time to move forward. No more tears, no more regrets and certainly no more guilt. After drying herself with one of Kate's luxurious bath towels, she moisturised her whole body with baby oil and threw on her most comfortable tracksuit.

'Wow that looks fantastic,' Gina exclaimed as she walked into the dining area.

The table was set with an expensive red tablecloth and matching napkins, lit candles and an open bottle of wine begging to be devoured.

'Woulda madame pleees bee seated?' Kate asked in a mock Greek accent, looking very pleased with herself. *'Isse there anytheeng I can getta madame?'* she continued as Gina sat down and poured them both a glass of wine.

'No thankyou, but I would like to know where you got that awful accent from? Anyone we know, by any chance?' Gina asked laughing. Kate opened up a napkin with an exaggerated flourish and placed it onto Gina's lap.

'Oh, no-one special,' she fibbed. 'Anyway, ugly sis, awaiting your pleasure is prawn cocktail to start, followed by my first attempt at moussaka and then ice-cream with chocolates, washed down by two bottles of white wine.'

The meal went down a treat and the wine quickly followed, resulting in an overwhelming fatigue borne of contentment. The hoped-for relaxation had been too successful and at 10.30pm they agreed that an early night was in order and all part of the medicinal process. Although Kieran was not there at weekends they continued to share the master bedroom as it did not occur to either of them to do anything different – they loved their chats just before they went to sleep. Tonight, they fell into bed chuckling at the size of their swollen stomachs before they kissed each other good night and settled down to sleep. After a few minutes of silence and while both of them were staring out into the darkness each with their own thoughts, a car pulled up and a crackling radio confirmed that it was a taxi bringing home some party-revellers. Male and female voices could be heard laughing and joking until they disappeared into a nearby house.

'I know we had lovely meal and a lovely evening,' sighed Gina, 'but I have to ask...'

'What sweetheart?' Kate answered sleepily as she snuggled further down trying to find a more comfortable position.

'What the hell are we doing in bed – with each other – this early on a Friday night?'

'Don't know,' Kate mumbled as she thumped her pillow indignantly. 'But don't worry about it. It ain't happening again.'

CHAPTER 10

It was Monday and Gina dropped Kieran off at school at 8.55 am which meant she was going to be late for work. Great, she thought to herself. On the very day that she wanted to ask her boss if there was any chance of a full-time position, she had to be late for the first time ever. Worse still was the fact that she had run out of ironed clothes and had not had time to do anything else but find the only reasonable looking outfit, which unfortunately equated to a worn-out dress that her mother would be embarrassed to wear. In fact, come to think of it, her mother had been embarrassed to wear it because she had given it to Gina in her last clear out. 'Oh God. I had all weekend to sort out my washing and what did I do?' she berated herself as she walked towards the bus stop. 'Never mind, no turning back now.'

Twenty minutes later, as she stepped into the office and took off her raincoat, there was a loud wolf whistle from Paul, the new accountant. He had joined the company from another branch a few weeks previously. This tall, dark newcomer with chiselled features, sky blue eyes and expensive tastes in clothes was the flavour of the month with the girls in the office. Most of the single ones had tried their luck with him but, so far, he had merely responded with amusement and some mild flirtation.

'Nice dress,' he remarked as he pulled a file out from his overhead cabinet and placed it onto his desk, looking up at her for a brief moment only.

'Do you think so?' Gina was bemused at this man's obvious lack of fashion knowledge – she thought she looked a mess. The wind had blown her hair over to one side of her head where it remained locked in position due to the amount of gel that she had hurriedly propelled into her curls, so she decided to check herself out in the mirror of the ladies bathroom. As she stepped inside her agitated expression was replaced with one of absolute horror as she could see that part of the hem at the back of her dress was tucked into the top of her panties, giving a glimpse of stocking tops and suspender clasps. Gina's hand went to her open mouth as she burst out laughing at the whole comical reflection. No wonder she had felt uncomfortable on the bus and no wonder Paul had thought it was a nice dress!

Paul was loitering when she emerged from the ladies and returned to her desk. He smiled again.

'I'm sorry Gina, that was really cheeky of me and I hope you weren't offended,' he offered his apologies in a near whisper and his blue eyes sparkled mischievously but with a look of sincere repentance.

'Well, I'm not sure what to think really, it wasn't very gentlemanly of you to wolf whistle. You could have been a bit more discreet instead of alerting the whole office to my underwear.'

'I really am truly sorry for such ungracious behaviour. Please let me buy you a drink to make up for it.'

'I'll think about it,' she replied nonchalantly, knowing full well that she was going to accept. Her heart beat wildly with anticipation as she finally acknowledged the chemistry that had been building up between them and the fact that her days in the office seemed more exciting than ever since Paul had joined the company. Was it only a few weeks? She felt as if she had known him forever and yet she knew nothing about him other than the fact he was looking to move into the area but in the meantime was staying in rented accommodation during the week, as a temporary measure. He often went away on business trips so they were only just beginning to get to know each other.

That evening she couldn't wait to tell Kate that Richard had agreed to her working full time and to ask her if she wouldn't mind babysitting while she went out for a drink with Paul on Wednesday.

*   *   *   *   *

Wednesday couldn't come soon enough for Gina. She had forgotten the magic of meeting up with someone for a first date and the excitement of preparing the body and mind over several days so that everything was perfect. It was a wonderful feeling and she savoured every moment by talking it through with Kate in detail.

'So you think my low-cut black dress with the split at the knee is fine for a Wednesday night, Kate?' she had asked more than once on Monday night.

'For the umpteenth time, yes,' answered Kate slowly while continuing to read the paper, one of two that they had delivered because they each refused to read the other's choice of newspaper due to their completely different political views.

'And even though Paul might not be taking me to a classy venue, you still think it'll be okay?' Gina asked biting her lip thoughtfully, oblivious to the fact that as far as Kate was concerned the subject was exhausted. Kate put the paper down onto the table,

'Gina,' she responded in her teacher-like voice. 'You are a beautiful woman with a body that some women would swop their multiple orgasms for so please, please will you stop torturing yourself – and me!'

'Okay, okay, I just wanted to be sure. But just one more thing.'

'So what is it now?' Kate said indulgently as she picked up the paper again and resumed reading the film reviews.

Gina put on her little girls' voice 'Will you please be a darling and give me a manicure and a pedicure tomorrow night. Pretty please?' she pleaded with her hands held together in mock prayer.

'What?' Kate shouted in feigned outrage, throwing the paper down onto her lap, 'And would you like me to peel some grapes for you at the same time?' she added haughtily. 'Oh, go on then, seeing as you're the best friend ever. One night of pampering in exchange for a favour from you.'
Gina clapped her hands together and smiled. 'Name your price.'

'That you stop leaving your bras in the bathroom. I don't want Mikos thinking he's missing out!' Kate laughed as she stuck her chest out and assumed a sulky pout.

When 8pm Wednesday finally arrived, Paul turned up at the doorstep of Kate's house to collect Gina in what Gina described as a 'very pretty red car'. Unlike Kate she had no hankering for a flash, expensive looking car and found Kate's enthusiasm for Ferraris and the like quite bewildering. But it didn't escape Kate's notice, as she looked out of her lounge window towards the road, that the pretty red car was in fact a Porsche and so Paul had already managed to impress her before he had even knocked on the front door.

'She won't be long,' she smiled at Paul as he held his hand out and introduced himself.

'Thanks,' he smiled back looking just a little nervous.

Hmmm, cute, thought Kate, just as Gina surfaced at the top of the staircase looking more incredible than Paul or Kate had ever seen her look before.

'Wow,' exclaimed Paul, who looked like the cat who'd got the cream. 'You look really gorgeous.' Gina returned his compliment with a dazzling smile that lit up the whole room as she glided down the stairs wearing the black dress. Her curls were swept up off her face and then tied loosely allowing them to cascade down her shoulders. Her silver shoes, handbag and jewellery completed a simple but elegant look that was sheer class. Gina felt on top of the world and it showed.

'Keep your hands to yourself tonight, young man,' Kate joked as they all walked to the front door.

'And bring her back in one piece, please.' But they didn't hear a word as they continued down the path with eyes only for each other.

They arrived at Tutti, the new Italian restaurant on the outskirts of the town, overlooking a beautiful lake that shimmered in the moonlight. Entering this highly reputed establishment helped to confirm that Gina had made the right decision on her attire and heads turned to stare at her as she was guided to the reserved table causing Paul to instinctively and proudly wrap a protective arm around her waist. Gina thought that this was going to be a memorable evening and her stomach fluttered again as she seated herself at the table and looked over at Paul.

'You look so handsome,' Gina blurted out before she could stop herself – *no game playing here then*, she thought, immediately chastising herself for allowing her private thoughts to escape. He didn't notice her momentary grimace as she squirmed inwardly.

'So do you, well I um, I mean you look beautiful and every man in this room wishes he were me at this precise moment.'

'Bet you say that to all the girls!' she giggled, feeling more at ease.

And so the evening began – light-hearted chatter that gradually became more personal and revealing, both sharing their innermost thoughts and fears as if they had known and trusted each other for years. Gina already knew that she wanted to see Paul again but there was one subject that had never been discussed before and she had to know before the relationship could go any further,

'Where is your ex-wife now?' Gina finally plucked up the courage to ask as she polished off her fourth glass of wine.

Paul's eyes widened, betraying that he was visibly taken aback, 'Oh, Emma is not my ex-wife yet, we're still married but she moved out of our house a few months back. She's still in Surrey but we don't speak much, except to discuss the sale of the house and my move to Cambridge.'

Gina nodded with empathy, wondering if Emma knew about her, but she didn't dare ask anything further for seeming too presumptuous and over keen, and so satisfied herself with the knowledge given. No children and a wife that was more than a hundred miles away equals an uncomplicated divorce and a free man. *That's good enough for me*, she thought.

After a wonderful meal and further bottle of wine, Gina accepted the offer of a nightcap and coffee at Paul's flat that was only a few miles from Kate's house. He had been lucky enough to secure a clean, modern two-bedroomed apartment, overlooking a park on one side and a quiet street on the other. As she looked around the lounge admiring his tidiness and good taste, the sexual tension between them began to mount and they both tried to ignore it by reverting back to small chatter. The delicious anticipation of what was to come, which for Gina was the first kiss and for Paul the hope that tonight Gina would finally be his, was more than both could bear. He had yearned for her body for so long now that he had never allowed himself to hope that making love to her could be a reality – until tonight – but was anxious not to frighten her off. Neither of them needed to dwell on their emotions for too long as the passions that had surfaced during the evening climaxed into a spontaneous embrace as they pulled each other close and as Gina's lips succumbed to Paul's gentle, tingling kissing, her heart raced. Every nerve in her body seemed to rise in readiness of his lovemaking. They were under each other's spell and there was no turning back. Paul's experienced hands stroked the top of Gina's shoulders as he brushed her hair from her face while continuing to kiss her, but now more passionately. His hands pulled down the straps of her dress and then the straps of her bra as he kissed her face and neck. Her voluptuous breasts were released in one smooth movement of his fingers and as he cupped them she gasped with pleasure. He tenderly led her into his bedroom and lay her on the bed where he kissed her body, in whispers, from her neck to her toes. She could bear it no longer and he eagerly obliged when she begged him to enter her. Their bodies became entwined in a passion that Gina had never experienced before and for the first time in many months she reached a climax that took her body and mind to a place she had forgotten existed, where pleasure becomes indescribable and the beginning of love emerges.

When it was all over, Gina curled her body against his and Paul held her tight, neither of them speaking.

Totally contented they fell asleep in moments.

CHAPTER 11

The package fell with a thump onto the doormat and woke everybody in the house. Gina put on her dressing gown and slippers to retrieve what she knew to be her first study pack for her correspondence course. She had agreed with Richard that she would study for a relevant qualification now that she was working full time and had opted for the accountancy route. After all, Paul could help her if she came across any difficult parts and at least he would have some understanding of what she would be going through, if at any time the whole thing became too stressful or time-consuming. As Paul seemed to be going away on business more and more these days it was sensible to start as soon as possible while she had the time.

As Kate reached the bottom stair, she leant on Gina's shoulders to see what had caught her attention.

'I take it that you've just received your mind-numbingly boring, couldn't think of a worse subject, school book that is going to propel you to a world rich with exciting numbers and equations?' Kate mocked, in between yawning and shuffling sleepily towards the kitchen.

'You'll be eating your words when I start raking in the money as a qualified accountant and wear designer labels that will make yours look like past times,' Gina responded without looking up but then with hands on hips she turned towards her friend and added. 'Excuse me, it's not a boring subject. It's quite fascinating if you must know.'

'Yeah, yeah, and so is watching a football match,' Kate shot back, filling the kettle and switching it on before returning to the sitting room.

'Oh nothing is as exciting as that,' Gina exclaimed as she finished unwrapping her parcel

'There's something wrong with you. Do you want coffee?'

'Yes please,' Gina replied gratefully. 'I'm going to miss your witty repartee when I move out next week.'

'Oh, I have no doubt about that. Toast or cereal?'

'Both please. Actually, joking apart, I will miss grown-up company for a while, but it'll also be nice being just Kieran and I.'

'Oh I don't suppose you'll be on your own for that long. I'm sure Paul has plans for the both of you.'

Gina frowned. 'I hope you're right but we mustn't be too presumptuous, at this stage. Paul's concentrating on his career at the moment and rightly so. I'm quite happy with the way things are, other than the fact he seems really stressed, but I'm sure that's down to the workload and travelling,' she said.

'I wouldn't worry too much. It's to be expected when a lot of travelling is involved. You know what hotels are like. Okay for a short time but on a regular basis it can be a lonely experience and a good nights sleep is about as likely as finding an unmarried attractive man with honourable intentions. Oops sorry, I'll go back to bed with my coffee and re-emerge without the shoulder chips, shall I?' Kate laughed as she shuffled her way back to the stairs.

'Good idea. You go back to bed and I'll cook us both a proper English breakfast.'

*   *   *   *   *

Sunday was spent quietly, Gina pouring over her assignments and Kate marking essays and preparing lesson plans. Although both girls worked hard, they did so at a leisurely pace, listening to background music and making the most of the peace and quiet that only a Sunday can offer.

When Joe arrived in the evening with Kieran, Gina asked Kate if she would take Kieran out into the kitchen for some tea, while she talked to her husband. Gina had dreaded the moment when she had to confront her mistakenly hopeful husband and felt that however much it was going to hurt all three of them, now was the right time to take away all his aspirations of a reunion.

Joe gave his son a big hug goodbye and then sat down expectantly, running his fingers through his hair and trying to smile. He had been hoping for this moment, when Gina told him that she wanted to start again and give him another chance. As she turned to face him and he saw the serious and determined expression on her face, his heart sank and his smile faded. You had to be an idiot to think it spelt anything other than bad news.

Gina explained as gently as she could that she had learnt much about herself during this time of separation and felt that life without him was the best option for her, Kieran and, in time, for everyone concerned. Although he may not be able to see that now, they were not good for each other any more, wanted different things and too much had happened for there to be any going back. Joe listened in silence, not saying a word, but his eyes displayed nothing short of total devastation as he slumped back into the chair. The words "we should think about getting a divorce" resonated in his ears as he slowly got up, kissed Gina on the cheek and walked out of the front door.

Gina burst into tears, her heart breaking at the sight of the defeated man she once loved walking away from her. She quickly composed herself to greet Kieran who was busily making a doorstep sandwich with an amazed Kate.

'Can this boy eat or what?' Kate asked, as she started to clear away the mess Kieran had made with the butter, cheese and coleslaw. 'This is his second you know. The first disappeared before I had a chance to ask "Would you like some pickle?" Still, you want to be a big, strong lad, don't you Kieran?' she smiled with affection as she ruffled his hair.

Kieran stood as tall as he could. 'Daddy told me that I need to eat lots, as I'm growing all the time, especially when I'm sleeping, so I wanted to make sure that I was full before I went to bed. And I ate all my vegetables today,' he finished.

'Okay darling, eat that and then I'll read you a story before you have your milk and brush your teeth.'

Kate put a reassuring hand on Gina's shoulder as she could tell quite easily that she was putting on a brave face. 'Don't worry, you've done the right thing and it'll get better in time, I promise,' she offered.

A few hours later there was an unexpected knock on the front door. Kate looked out of her window.

'Oh no,' she moaned at the uninvited interruption.

'Who is it?' asked an anxious Gina jumping up from her horizontal position on the all too-comfy sofa.

'I hate to tell you this, but it's Joe and he looks a little worse for wear. There's no way that we're answering that door,' Kate said moving swiftly away from the window but Joe had already spotted her face through the curtains.

'Gina, Gina. I need to see you,' he shouted through the letterbox. 'Open the door, please. I just want to talk to you,' he added desperately.

'He won't go away Kate so you might as well let him in. I can promise you that he'll cause a scene until you do. Are you sure he's been drinking?'

'Well, he can hardly stand up. Does that answer your question? You'd better make yourself scarce. Go on quickly, go upstairs and lock yourself in our room – I'll deal with this,' Kate ordered, ushering her towards the stairs. Gina dashed up to their bedroom pausing at Kieran's door. He was fast asleep so she closed the door fully to protect him from any possible discord.

Once Kate was sure that Gina was safely locked in, she opened the door to Joe who practically fell onto the floor as he tried to push pass Kate. 'Where is she?' he asked loudly. 'I want to speak to my wife and I want to speak to her now.'

Kate stood firm in front of him, blocking his way. 'She's not available Joe, but you can talk to me. Come into the kitchen and I'll make you a drink.'

He followed her without saying a word.

'Coffee?' she asked patiently, and if she was at all fearful it wasn't obvious. She closed the kitchen door and as she prepared the cups for coffee she continued. 'Why have you come round to my house drunk? You know this won't solve anything and if Kieran wakes up and gets caught in the middle of your marriage problems, she'll never forgive you. This is not the way to solve things. You know that, don't you?'

Joe leant against the fridge to stop the swaying and just stared at Kate. He looked pathetic but Kate was determined not to feel sorry for him and continued to make the coffee. 'Well Joe? Am I making sense? Speak to me, please,' she demanded gently as she tried to hand him the mug of drink. But there were no words, no solutions and no cure that could be offered, and he just shook his head. Waving the drink away, he sank into a heap on the floor and burst into tears. It had been a long time since Kate had watched a grown man cry and she really didn't know what to do. Slowly she sat beside him on the floor and tentatively put her arms around him, allowing him to sob until the tears ran dry. She assured him that he could see Gina another day soon when he was feeling stronger and wasn't influenced by alcohol. This seemed to calm him down and, embarrassed by his behaviour, he kissed Kate on the cheek and apologised. Before he left he made her promise that she would tell Gina that he loved her and would prove to her that he really could change and win her back. Kate said that he could tell her himself another time and offered to phone for a taxi. Joe refused and left quietly by the back door. The whole incident had left Kate emotionally drained and now she could also see why Gina had taken so long to leave her husband. Nobody is all bad, she thought, some just need a lot of help and reassurance to release them from their confusion and inner turmoil.

Kate went upstairs to tell Gina that it was safe and that he had gone. 'He *will* be alright. You do know that, don't you?'

Gina nodded miserably and wiped away her own tears with her fingertips.

Kate continued, 'Well, I've got one hug left from today's quota,' she joked. 'Would you like it now or later?'

Gina smiled through her dried tears. 'I'll take it now, if you don't mind. Before somebody else knocks on the front door.'

CHAPTER 12

Gina moving in with Kate had always been a temporary arrangement, but when Gina had first started to look for her own place Kate was disappointed. Not only had she really enjoyed having her friend living with her, she had also provided the perfect excuse for Kate to keep her distance with Mikos. Hurt takes a long time to heal and Kate needed to be sure of Mikos before she allowed him to get too close to her. However, as every woman knows, you can't dictate to your heart, it dictates to you, and by the time Gina had moved out Kate was hopelessly in love.

It was the Friday following Gina's departure that Kate invited Mikos over for dinner. He had been his usual prompt self, arriving with an enormous bouquet of flowers. Those first few moments together had been somewhat awkward. Kate busied herself in the kitchen, arranging her flowers in a crystal vase and checking on the progress of dinner. She poured herself and Mikos a drink and joined him on the sofa. The tension between them was electric and as they looked into each other's eyes their desire for each other was palpable. No words were necessary. They fell into each other's arms and began kissing hungrily and passionately. They began to strip frantically as they climbed the stairs, clawing at each other as their desire for each other reached fever pitch. They fell onto the bed naked and he entered her immediately, their need for each other so strong. Once their initial desire had been sated, Mikos started to make love to Kate slowly and gently. He kissed her neck, her nipples, her arms, her stomach, slowly devouring her and taking in the sweet scent of her soft smooth skin. He moved down to between her legs, caressing her with his tongue and slowly seeking out her core. Kate writhed as he found her most intimate spot and slowly waves of pure pleasure began to waft through her entire body, growing and growing in intensity until she finally screamed out for him. He entered her again but this time he was slow and sensual. They began to move in unison as though they had always been together. Again the waves of pure pleasure began to soar through Kate's body and as she arched towards him his own passion matched hers. They moved together, absorbing each other totally, the waves growing stronger and stronger until finally they reached the peak of their desire together, and their passion for each other exploded at the same time, totally devouring them both. They lay together for the longest time, arms around each other, savouring the beauty of the moment, words totally unnecessary.

Eventually Kate slid off the bed and disappeared from the bedroom, returning shortly with their dinner on a tray. As they picnicked on the bed together, still naked, they laughed and joked and revelled in the sheer debauchery of their actions. Mikos was serious only for a short while when he admitted to Kate that he had fallen in love with her and proclaimed that making love to her that night had been a totally religious experience.

That night Kate slept more soundly than she had ever slept before, locked in the arms of the man she loved and who loved her back. They spent the entire weekend alone together in Kate's house, satisfying their hunger for each other in the bedroom and their physical hunger with take-away deliveries. On the Sunday they talked about Mikos moving in as if it were *a fait-accomplis* and agreed that after work on Monday Mikos would go back to his flat and pack his things before returning. And so it was. Mikos returned the Monday evening with what looked to Kate to be little more than a weekend bag, but he assured her that it contained all that he needed.

That week was wonderful. Now that their long courtship and love for each other had found a physical outlet, their desire for each other was uncontrollable. After their days at work, Mikos would prepare a meal while Kate did her following day's preparation. They would go to bed early, not so Kate could get her beauty sleep but so they could enjoy and devour each other physically. Their love- making was passionate and insatiable and Kate was convinced that she had finally found the right man. She even blushed when she was explaining to her 'O' level students how Lady Chatterly's passion and desire for her husband's gamekeeper overrode all her common sense and feelings of foreboding for the future.

The following Saturday Mikos had to work and Kate had arranged to meet Gina for coffee. They met at their usual café. It was the place they had gone to when they had first met up again. They returned to it to console each other when their lives were desperate and they met there to plot and scheme their return to normality. So it seemed appropriate that it should now be the venue to celebrate their happiness. Kate enthused about her new life with Mikos, how she had never been happier, or more exhausted, and they laughed like drains as Kate theatrically relayed how in the bedroom she was a truly religious experience. Gina for her part was equally happy. She and Kieran had settled into their new home, her new job was going well and on the romantic front, things with Paul were looking very promising. Gina explained that her recent concerns about Paul's pre-occupation with other matters had subsided and he had returned to his former attentive self, concluding that it must have been merely work pressures. Again, the two women struggled with their laughter as Kate mocked Gina for her less than subtle approach at attracting a man.

'Well of course men will notice you if you flash your knickers at them.' Their time together had flown by and reluctantly they agreed that they must part as they both had things to do.

'It's been great seeing you Gina, I'll give you a call soon, I promise. Now take care and be gentle with Paul,' Kate mocked as they kissed each other goodbye.

'You likewise with Mikos, young Katherine. Stay this happy,' and then added more seriously. 'And Kate, be careful.'

What made Gina add those last few words Kate couldn't comprehend, and even if she had asked Gina outright, she wouldn't have been able to explain either. But they played on Kate's mind as she wandered around the supermarket doing her weekly grocery shop. Gina had set off a warning bell and the pragmatic Kate couldn't fail to listen. She couldn't ignore the lessons she had learnt from her past and instinctively knew that she must safeguard her future. That night she would ask Mikos to sign a disclaimer to her property and her belongings. He knew about her past and would see that she was just being cautious. She was sure he would understand, he loved her and would do this to make her feel happy and more secure. In any case, it would become null and void when they married and so it was only a temporary arrangement anyway. Once Kate had reasoned all this in her mind she again felt calm and more confident. She hurried home to complete the housework, prepare a meal and await Mikos' return.

It was over dinner that Kate broached the subject and relayed the speech she had practised in the supermarket, looking at him expectantly as she finished.

'Of course I understand, darling, I would do anything for you,' he said reassuringly as he face softened into his usual persuasive grin.

Kate's eyes moistened at the gentleness in his voice.

'I do love you Mikos, and I do trust you. It's just that what with everything that's happened to me before I met you….'

She trailed off as Mikos interrupted. 'There's no need to explain further my darling, I understand. It's not a problem. Just get it organised and I'll sign whatever you want me to. Now let's forget it and finish this delicious meal you've cooked before it gets cold.' And with that they returned to their usual relaxed companionship.

After dinner while they were relaxing on the sofa Mikos checked his cigarette packet and commented that he was nearly out.

'I'll just pop to the corner shop and get some more and I'll pick up a bottle of wine as well,' he smiled as he slipped on his shoes and kissed her on the cheek. 'Do you need any?'

'No I'm fine, I got a carton this afternoon, see you in a minute,' Kate responded as she snuggled down on the sofa and continued to watch the romantic comedy on the television.

It must have been nearly a half hour before Kate realised that Mikos had been gone a long time. She got up and looked out of the window but saw nothing but a deserted street. She sat down again to continue to watch the film but couldn't concentrate; her unease was growing more and more. As time went on her imagination began to get the better of her as she pictured him in the road, a victim of a hit and run accident. She grabbed her keys and, after slipping on her shoes, left the house to retrace his steps. She saw nothing but as she returned to the house she noticed that his car had gone. The panic inside her began to rise and once back inside, not knowing what else to do, she phoned Gina.

'Gina, its me can you talk?' Kate asked surprising herself at how calm she sounded.

'Yes I'm bloody alone tonight. Paul's had to go away on business – yet again.'

Gina's frustration did not register with Kate as she continued. 'You're not going to believe this. Mikos popped out for a packet of cigarettes two hours ago and hasn't come back.'

Gina roared with laughter.

'Don't laugh, this is serious. He's taken the car and disappeared,' Kate shouted hysterically at her friend.

Realising how distraught Kate was Gina apologised profusely. ' Sorry, really sorry. Sit tight, I'm on my way.'

Gina was at Kate's side within minutes and, after phoning Accident and Emergency and the Police station to confirm that nothing had happened to Mikos, she spent the night with her friend, trying to comfort her through this bizarre and inexplicable nightmare.

*   *   *   *   *

How Kate got through the next few weeks she'll never know. She spent endless hours with Gina analysing *ad-infinitum* his mysterious disappearance. She escaped to Surrey to stay with Sandie and David at every opportunity. She even visited the garage where Mikos worked on several occasions. Always she had just missed him, he'd left early or gone to collect a car or something similar, and cryptic comments from his colleagues about her being the most attractive debt collector they'd ever come across, only deepened the mystery.

Kate was so irritated by her last failed attempt to see him that her frustrations got the better of her. Feeling guilty and embarrassed she phoned Gina to confess.

'Gina, I've done something really stupid,' she admitted in a pathetic voice.

'Go on,' Gina asked picking up the telephone cradle and moving towards her favourite armchair.

Hearing the apprehension in Gina's voice, Kate continued with renewed defiance. 'But I feel really good in spite of it.'

'Just tell me, Kate.' Gina demanded impatiently.

Kate took a deep breath. 'Well, I spotted his car in the forecourt and in front of all the other car mechanics, I let out the air from all of his tyres!'

'You didn't!' Gina exclaimed, relieved that it was nothing more than a minor prank.

'Oh yes I did but I knew that he'd be able to pump them up really easily. A bit immature I know,' she giggled feeling proud now. 'But it made me feel so much better and I really wanted to annoy him.'

'Didn't they try and stop you?' Gina asked as she flung her legs over the arm of her chair and rested her head with a wry smile.

'No they didn't. In fact they stood there laughing. I got the impression that they were enjoying it too, so they must also think he's a scumbag.'

'Good for you Kate but I think you may have been a bit too easy on the bastard – I would've slashed them!' she exaggerated in an endeavour to make her friend feel vindicated.

'No you wouldn't Gina but thanks for your support. I was feeling guilty until I spoke to you, now I feel positively righteous!'

*   *   *   *   *

It was several weeks later, one Wednesday evening, while marking some English essays, that Kate's doorbell rang suddenly. She opened it, expecting to dismiss an unwanted double-glazing salesman, but was stopped short. On her doorstep was a young woman, brunette and slight and who would have been attractive had she not looked so drawn and ill.

'Hello, I'm sorry to disturb you but I'm Debbie, Mikos' fiancée, and I've heard he's living here now. Can I speak to him please?'

Kate saw the effort that was required by this young woman to utter these words, and her heart went out to her.

'I'm sorry but he's not here, he hasn't been for several weeks, but do come in for a moment. Can I get you something?' Kate offered as she saw the look of total despair on the young woman's face.

She nodded as she entered hesitantly and sat down where Kate indicated. Kate made two coffees and sat down near her, curiosity almost exploding within her.

'I'm sorry, but I don't quite understand….' Kate started, but was interrupted as Debbie broke down and relayed a story so similar to hers that it made her blood boil.

Debbie had met Mikos at a nightclub. He had swept her off her feet and she had fallen madly in love with him. He was a real gentleman who had courted her slowly and extravagantly and had eventually asked her to marry him. They had begun to look for a house together and had quickly found the perfect home for them both. He had dealt with all the paperwork; all she had to do was withdraw her five thousand pounds life savings for the deposit. She had handed it over to him one lunch hour and returned to work while he went off to see the mortgage arranger. Or so she thought. That was the last she saw of him. She had since found out that he owed a lot of money to a lot of people, some of them quite suspect. She didn't think he was a conman but an extravagant soul who had got into a spot of bother. She wanted to find him and tell him it was all okay, that they could sort out his debts together and try again.

Kate smiled sympathetically at this young woman's naivety; she looked at that moment little more than a girl who still believed in happy endings. Kate relayed her own story in an effort to convince her to cut her losses and move on but was sure that as she left she would continue her fruitless search for Mikos and her elusive fantasy.

On the phone to Gina afterwards, once Kate had recounted the details of her surreal evening caller, she thanked her lucky stars for her narrow escape. However, deep down Kate's heart was breaking all over again and although she was trying hard to hide the fact from Gina, with her upbeat banter, she knew that she was not fooled and that Gina recognised that her friend was again deeply unhappy.

CHAPTER 13

This particular Saturday seemed like any other ordinary day when Gina left her house to pop into the supermarket. However, this was not her usual supermarket, as she had already completed her weekly shop the night before. Her mother had rung her this morning to ask if she would pick up a prescription drug from the pharmacy, as her father had forgotten to do so and was now out playing golf and wasn't that just typical of a man with golf on the brain? Gina did not mind at all as it gave her a chance to spend some time with her mother, without the distraction of any of the male species in the family. Little did she know that this favour was about to produce a not-so-ordinary day.

Life is full of coincidences and Gina often pondered on whether there was such a thing as coincidence or if fate maps out everybody's life down to the very last small detail. Gina was about to examine this very issue sooner than she'd thought.

She entered the supermarket feeling uncomfortably untidy, having not bothered to shower or put on any make up due to the fact that her mother was in pain and the sooner she collected the painkillers, the better. As she made her way through the various aisles to reach the pharmacy at the back, she spotted who she thought was Paul at the delicatessen counter. But how could it be when he lived miles away and had told her he was too busy to stay over last night?

It didn't take her long to establish that it was indeed Paul and her heart missed a beat with excitement and trepidation. Her first thought was to hide away – he had yet to see her without any make-up – but this was surpassed by her curiosity as to why he was here in the first place. He had his back turned towards her and she was just about to call out his name when a tall, attractive blond woman, who seemed to appear from nowhere, was at his side. If there was ever a moment of hope in which Gina dismissed her as a friend or a sister, it quickly evaporated when this woman lovingly put her arm around his waist and kissed him gently on the cheek, whispering something in his ear that made him burst out laughing. Seeing him so happy with another woman was truly heartbreaking and Gina was frozen to the spot as she tried to take in this alien scene which had unfolded in front of her. Gina composed herself and quickly moved out of the way so that there was no chance of him seeing her. There was nothing she could do about it now and, although it was going to totally wreck her whole weekend, she would have to wait until Monday to find out what was going on.

*   *   *   *   *

Sandie had decided that she and Kate should go out without David for a change, to catch up with each other's news including an in depth discussion about what was now known as "The Greek Episode".

It so happened that there was a party that Sandie had been invited to and David was more than happy for Kate to take his place.

They arrived at the beautiful Georgian house, set in wonderful Surrey countryside, at 8pm exactly and Kate was welcomed immediately by the attractive hostess, Diana, who was celebrating her fortieth birthday along with her husbands forty-fifth.

'Please come in, you're one of the first to arrive,' she said as she opened the door wide allowing the view of the hallway to be seen. She kissed the air either side of Sandie's cheeks and extended her hand out to Kate in an almost royal manner offering only her fingers for a handshake. She then turned and glided across the floor of the huge entrance hall and into the living area.

'Let me introduce you to the few that are already inside and have started on the champers,' she said.

Promising start, thought Kate, never one to turn down a good glass of champagne.

'This is Harvey, he has a farm up the road,' Diana explained as Harvey inclined his head in a small dignified manner. 'And this is Paula, Carol and Emma, my best friends,' she added, waving a long-fingered, overly manicured and adorned hand at the trio. 'You have to be a best friend to arrive at a party this early, don't you think?' she asked and, without waiting for an answer, concluded. 'And this is John, my husband, so hands off this one – he's all mine.' She laughed out loudly as she squeezed his cheek between her forefinger and thumb. John smiled meekly and acknowledged the guests by gesturing that he would take their jackets.

Kate took an instant dislike to Diana and, realising why David had given up his place so graciously, inwardly smiled. She also found Harvey a rather strange looking fellow, with his dry blond hair, tweed jacket, cord trousers and his large red bulbous nose. Carol and Paula had been slightly offhand when they were being introduced so she decided to avoid them as best she could. Feeling uncomfortable she followed Sandie into the kitchen, for that all-important first drink, as Diana continued talking at them. Kate downed the first glass of champagne in one go. She then took a deep breath and poured herself a second before plucking up the courage to join the rest of the party revellers. She was immediately drawn to Emma, a pretty blond, who had been sitting quietly and elegantly while the others continued to chat about themselves, laughing all the time at Harvey's jokes that were not really funny at all. Kate joined Emma on a beautiful cream leather sofa that was set apart from the rest of the room by a large ornate Chinese rug.

'So how do you know each other?' Kate asked her, not hiding the fact that she didn't think the others would be her cup of tea by glancing almost haughtily in their direction.

'Oh, I don't know them that well really. They're friends of Diana and I only see them when she has one of her birthday bashes. I only know Diana because our husbands are on the same cricket team and we organise the refreshments together.' Emma smiled, conveying to Kate that she understood the real meaning behind her question.

'That makes more sense,' Kate replied as she pulled an ashtray towards her. 'I take it we can smoke here?'

Emma nodded, 'And what about you? How do you know Sandie?'

'We go back a long way to our University days. Let's just say it's a few good years. We've remained firm friends ever since, even though Sandie married David and moved away.'

'So you don't live round here, then?'

No, Cambridge,' Kate answered, noticing that Harvey was starting to give her the eye. She moved her body round towards Emma so as to avoid any further of his come on looks but she could feel him staring at the back of her head and it made her shudder.

'Cambridge?' Emma said clapping her hands excitedly. 'What a coincidence. I was there only last night with my husband and I loved it. If it hadn't been for the fact that I'd promised Diana I would come to her party, I wouldn't have left there this morning. It's a fantastic City.'

'Yes it is. Romantic weekend?'

'Something like that. Paul and I separated a few months ago and he moved to Cambridge but we've recently decided to give it another go – I'm thinking of moving up there and it's great that I'll already have someone I know to turn to if Paul doesn't behave.'

Kate only half listened to the rest of Emma's story. Could this possibly be Gina's Paul? No, surely that would be too much of a coincidence, wouldn't it? How could she find out? Ask a few questions, dimwit.

Emma continued looking totally comfortable imparting information to a total stranger, 'And after his last affair I said I would never forgive him but I just love him so much. I'm far more miserable without him than I am with him. He makes me feel so alive.'

'So where is he now?' Kate managed to hide the turmoil of her thoughts and her feeling of surreal confusion. 'Will he be joining us at one point tonight?'

'Oh no, unfortunately he has things to do, now that his plans have changed. He's spending the rest of weekend looking at some houses and compiling a short list for my next trip to Cambridge and I too have things to do here tomorrow. It's so exciting and I can't believe my luck that you're here to tell me all about the city I'm going to be living in. Please, I want to hear all there is to know,' Emma pleaded, her face glowing with happiness.

The two continued, with Kate asking questions until she knew without doubt that Emma and Gina were in love with the same Paul. Kate could not do anything until the next day as her friend was expecting her to stay the whole weekend. No, she would brave it out until the morning when she would drive straight to Gina's house to break the terrible news. Kate spent the rest of the evening avoiding Harvey and putting on a happy face and there was nothing but relief when Sandie asked Kate if she was ready to leave.

*   *   *   *   *

Gina was not looking her best when Kate arrived at her house at 11am the next day. She was still in her dressing gown when she opened her front door. Her pale face lit up on seeing Kate, just when she needed her the most, but the smile was replaced by a concerned frown when she saw her expression.

'What on earth has happened Kate? You look terrible. Come in, come in,' she beckoned, turning her thoughts away from her own worries as all sorts of nasty images flashed before her. 'Have you had some bad news?'

'Well you could say that. I don't know where to begin, I really don't Gina.'

'In your own time. Let me get you a drink.'

Kate waited until they were both sat comfortably with coffee and cigarettes, as she knew it was going to be a long session. She proceeded to explain everything to Gina, as kindly as she knew how, and hugged her closely when Gina began to cry. There was no ranting and raving or name-calling. Just tears gently rolling down her cheeks as she then told Kate about the supermarket incident and how unlucky Paul was to get caught out in such an amazingly coincidental way. After accepting the reality of what these two incidents meant, it wasn't long before they were plotting his downfall, which went from the sublime to the ridiculous and eventually had them rolling about with laughter.

The next morning, after taking Kieran to school, Gina set off for work with a face like thunder. Her emotions had gone from resigned to angry, then determined and finally back to anger in just a few minutes. A part of her couldn't wait to get into the office to have a go at Paul but her heart was trying to find a way out from the lies, excuses and deceit – something that meant it was all a misunderstanding and everything was going to be alright after all. Although she knew deep down that the pieces of the jigsaw had been put together, she still hoped that perhaps she had been looking at the wrong puzzle.

As she entered the building she could feel her defense mechanisms clunk into position as she smiled at the receptionist and wished her a good morning.

'Good morning, Gina. Nice weekend?'

'Fabulous thank-you Ann. And you?' she replied convincingly without stopping for an answer.

As she reached the top of the first flight of stairs, she could see that Paul was in the kitchen making the teams first hot drink of the day and she took a deep breath. *Take it easy, give him time to explain and be calm*, she told herself. Paul turned to look at Gina and in that instant she knew. The body language, his eyes and the expression on his face told her everything she needed to know. She didn't even give him time to verbally acknowledge her presence.

'When were you going to tell me then, Paul?' she whispered loudly into his ear as she reached up to grab a cup from the kitchen cupboard. Paul was startled at the venom in her voice and turned to look at her, watching her as she threw a tea bag and some sugar into her favourite Ipswich Town mug. *She couldn't know about Emma surely?* he thought.

Gina stirred her drink and threw the spoon down hard into the sink. 'I know all about Emma, you cheating bastard,' she said quietly as she looked deep into his eyes so that he would understand how angry she truly was. 'Anything you'd like to say to me, then, Paul? No I thought not. I suggest you stay away from me for as long as you possibly can today as I really can't give you any guarantees on how I might behave.'

She stormed out of the room and left Paul speechless as he his mind raced, trying to fathom how she had managed to find out about Emma before he'd had the chance to let her down gently. He thought he had been so careful and not even his parents knew the latest development. The rest of the day saw them both avoid one another until he could bear it no longer.

'I'm so sorry Gina, I was going to tell you when I'd plucked up the courage. How did you find out?'

Without looking up from her desk she answered. 'It's a small world, Paul, especially in Surrey. Let's just say that someone or something made sure that I saw you very clearly. Please leave me alone for a few days and then perhaps we may be able to talk about being work colleagues again.'

Paul was none the wiser but, grateful for the easy option, just nodded and walked away.

CHAPTER 14

On finishing her day at the school Kate made her way to Gina's house, complete with a bottle of wine and her weekend bag. Kieran saw Kate pull up outside his new home and rushed downstairs to greet her shouting, 'Mummy, mummy, Kates here, so can we go out for tea now?'

'Give Kate a chance to say hello first please Kieran,' she smiled as she opened her front door.

'That's a nice greeting, young man,' exclaimed Kate smiling, pleasantly surprised by his enthusiasm.

'Don't flatter yourself Kate, he's just very hungry! He's not used to waiting this long for his tea.'

'Thanks for shattering my illusions. I thought I could still excite at least one member of the opposite sex. Never mind. What's it to be then Kieran – burger or nuggets?'

'Oh, I haven't had time to tell you,' replied Gina. 'Or perhaps Kieran should. Go on darling, tell Kate where you would like to eat.'

Kieran looked at Kate very seriously. In his most grown up voice he said, 'I don't eat animals anymore,' and went on to explain that yesterday he went on a school visit to a farm and decided that he was only ever going to eat vegetables, from now on.

'Got any ideas? Gina asked as she accepted Kate's bottle of wine and ushered Kieran into the living area. 'Because I haven't got a clue.'

'I'm not into nut cutlets or pretend meat so how about a pizza?' Kate enthused.

All agreed that this was the best option and set off for the best pizza restaurant on offer to enjoy each other's company before Kieran spent the weekend with his dad.

After a lovely meal in which Kieran revelled in the attentions of two adoring females, they drove to Joe's flat and left a happy boy to enjoy the weekend with his dad. Gina asked Kate if they could forego the quick drink they had planned and return home, as she was not in the mood for crowds. Kate did not mind at all and in fact had expected Gina to want just her company this evening. They agreed that a shopping trip the next day would be much more therapeutic than drowning any sorrows.

After spending Saturday morning half-heartedly window-shopping they chose an intimate bistro in which to satisfy their growing hunger, having given up on finding anything that tempted them to part with their hard earned money.

The subdued lighting and relaxed ambience of the bistro gave them the perfect excuse to wile away the afternoon savouring each other's company rather than trying to fill the day with various pointless distractions.

'You're such a bad influence Kate and I'll be blaming you if I fail my exams. I really should be at home studying instead of indulging my stomach again,' Gina said, popping an olive into her mouth.

'I've got every faith in you making up the time and in any case your studying will be far more productive if you're well fed. That's my philosophy anyway,' Kate replied as she perused the menu. 'I think I'll go for the fish, it will leave room for a desert,' she added pensively.

'Stop talking about food for one moment,' Gina lowered her voice and touched Kate's hand as it rested on the menu. 'We've both been through a bad time recently but I can't help noticing that you seem pre-occupied just lately. Is something worrying you, Kate? If it's me you're concerned about then you needn't be, because I really am fine without Paul, especially now that he's left the company. In fact, I've decided I don't need a man at all at the moment.'

'Well I do,' Kate admitted churlishly. 'It's okay for you, you've got Kieran, but time is running out for me. I want children, Gina, and a good husband with a nice home. I want a happy family life where I can give up worrying about my career and concentrate on what's really important in life.'

Gina was taken aback by the intensity of her tone. 'Gosh I didn't realise that you were that desperate to settle down. You've still got plenty of time and your body clock's got loads of mileage left.' At this, Kate reached over to the paper napkin, neatly folded in her wineglass, and used it to wipe the tears that she'd been trying to hold back for most of the day.

'I'm sorry Gina, I didn't mean to spoil our day out. Must be the hormones.'

Gina listened intently as Kate explained that she felt empty inside and that her life seemed to have a big hole that couldn't be filled with her day to day being. Her yearning for a child was taking over her thoughts, and her need to be loved by a man was so profound that she didn't think she would ever be happy again.

'Where are all the good men?' she asked Gina. 'We always seem to find the bastards and the older I get, the harder it seems to find a decent man with no baggage. I'm fed up with unpacking it all and then watching them disappear, rebuilt and raring to go again, leaving me with all the nasty debris. I really am. Anyway, enough about that, are you sure you're alright now?' At this point the waiter arrived to take their order, took one look at them both and walked away again.

'Oh well, you've managed to frighten this one off Kate and I'd rather you hadn't. This one brings food and that's good enough for me at the moment!' Gina laughed and this made Kate smile. 'And don't worry, there's someone just round the corner for you. I can feel it in my water. You're going to find a lovely, generous knight in the obligatory shining armour. You've got everything going for you and you may not realise this but I envy you too.'

'You do?' Kate had stopped crying completely now.

'Uh uh. You've got a great career, your own home that you can easily afford and freedom to do what you want, when you want. I have to put Kieran first all the time and I still live with the terrible guilt that he no longer lives with both his parents. It's taking me much longer to get over that than I ever imagined. But I'll get there. And so will you, I promise.'

Gina beckoned towards the waiter to let him know it was now safe to approach them, which he duly did. As he hovered near their table Kate gave him one of her biggest smiles, as if to make amends for embarrassing him.

'And you can leave him alone Kate,' Gina commanded jokingly, once he had left with their order. 'You've got tights that are older than him!'

'Spoil sport,' Kate said, back on form and feeling more positive. Gina always kept her promises. She was sure she was right and it was just a matter of being patient.

PART TWO

AN
EMOTIONAL
JOURNEY

CHAPTER 15

It had been such a hot summer's night that Kate had been forced to get up to open her bedroom curtains and windows wide to try and get as much air as possible to circulate. When the sun, streaming into her bedroom, woke her this Saturday morning, Kate still felt tired. She wasn't sure whether it was the heat that had kept her awake or the anticipation of tonight's party. In any event, she decided she would have a lazy day and save her energy for tonight and, with that thought, she turned over and went back to sleep. When she woke a couple of hours later, she checked her bedside clock and realised she'd better get up, before she progressed from the merely decadent to the total slovenly.

After her customary coffee and cigarette, she quickly washed and then proceeded to make a meat dish for that evening. Tonight's bash was to be a barbecue with every guest having been asked to bring along a dish. Kate had decided upon Teriyaki beef, an exotic far-eastern recipe given to her by Sandie, with which she hoped to impress. She then relaxed over her sandwich lunch with the daily newspaper before deciding to treat herself to a full pampering session in preparation for tonight.

As she lay in the hot, sweetly scented bubble bath she closed her eyes and let her mind wander. Inevitably it turned to the only area in her life which hadn't worked out as she'd envisaged – her love life. Finding out about the true nature of Mikos had been very therapeutic for Kate. She had moved on from broken-hearted and miserable to anger very quickly. This had subsided to relief at her lucky escape just as quickly. In fact, the entire sorry little episode with Mikos, coupled with her previous experiences had made her all the more strong. She smiled inwardly as she sunk deeper into the bubbles.

She had recently found contentment in being alone. She was happy with her single life. She had realised she was much better off by herself than with the wrong man. Her desire to be a part of a couple had blinded her to certain realities in the past and she had chosen to overlook certain failings in men. Now, for the first time ever, she appreciated the benefits of a single life-style: the calmness, the routine, the control and the lack of an emotional roller coaster. If the right man came along, she realised, she'd have these still and if he didn't, then she'd continue to appreciate them alone. It was with this new-found philosophy that Kate now faced the world.

After Kate emerged from her bath she indulged herself with every beauty treatment she had to hand: facemask, exfoliation, manicure, pedicure and moisturising. In fact, by the time she had finished she had used nearly every tube and jar in her bathroom cabinet. She then applied her make-up, styled her hair and got dressed in a pair of tight grey suede jeans and matching top before driving over to Gina's.

Kate dropped her overnight bag in the hallway before taking the glass of wine proffered by Gina.

'Nervous?' Gina queried.

'No. Why, should I be?' Kate answered with as much calm as she could muster.

'Don't play the innocent with me, my girl, you've been waiting for this opportunity for ages.'

'I know, but with my luck nothing will transpire.'

'What do you mean exactly? Your luck with men generally or with this one in particular?' Gina continued.

Kate smiled ruefully. 'Either, both,' she answered. 'I mean, if I ever do get anywhere with him, he'll probably turn out to be as big a cad as every other man I've ever got entangled with. But if the past few months are anything to go by, nothing is going to happen anyway.'

'Don't be so pessimistic,' Gina countered. 'At least we now know he's not married or gay.'

'Don't remind me. Are we still that naïve we assume that simply because a man doesn't flirt with everything in a skirt he has to be either married or gay?'

They both laughed at their initial assumption when Max had first walked into the wine bar and Kate had been instantly drawn to him. She couldn't believe how engrossed in conversation he was with his friends and how totally oblivious he appeared to what was going on around him. Over the next few weeks and months whenever they spotted him on their regular nights out, Kate did her utmost to attract his attention, but to no avail. On one occasion as he sat chatting to a friend at the bar, she even pushed her way in-between them, stopping their conversation, to order drinks. Gina nearly choked on her wine as she watched in humorous disbelief. Still he appeared not to notice her. They were veering towards concluding he was gay when one week his group arrived with the addition of a tall attractive brunette who appeared to be very comfortable and at ease with him. His wife, or at the very least his long-term girlfriend, Kate had concluded somewhat dejectedly. Then last week, while out, they had bumped into a colleague of Kates', out with her friends, one of whom was the tall attractive brunette, Louise. She turned out to be the sister of Max, who was single, unattached and straight, and whom Louise wanted to see settle down. Kate's colleague, Stephanie, finding out that Kate was attracted to Max, then invited her and Gina to her birthday barbecue the following week.

And that is how Kate and Gina found themselves here this Saturday night eagerly awaiting a birthday bash. They decided on another glass of wine before ordering the taxi, as Kate needed a little more Dutch courage and also she didn't want to appear overly eager by arriving too early. When they arrived at the party Louise and Max were there and, on seeing them, Louise welcomed them extravagantly while Max immediately coloured from the neck up. Louise admitted she had been teasing Max all day to the extent that he nearly didn't come.

Great, thought Kate, heavy with sarcasm. *She's probably ruined any chance I may have had.*

However, her mother had often relayed the old adage "the way to a man's heart was through his stomach" which was why Kate had so meticulously prepared the Teriyaki beef. She immediately went to the barbecue, cooked the beef and then offered it around. It was a great success and Kate felt very pleased that Max had obviously enjoyed it. *At least he knows I can cook,* she thought to herself.

But once everyone had finished eating the large array of food on offer and the party began to get going in earnest, Kate felt extremely self conscious. She was well aware of Max's glances in her direction and she was also aware that he was conscious of her glances towards him. Louise's admission of teasing Max had made her feel awkward and so instead of positioning herself advantageously she stayed at the opposite end of the room. This conscious ignoring of one another went on for what seemed like hours and while Kate and Max became increasingly tense the rest of the guests found it immensely amusing. In desperation Gina finally went over to talk to Louise in a very conspiratorial manner.

'Max,' Louise called. 'Could you come over here a minute. We need your advice.'

Max walked over with a slightly suspicious look in his eyes.

'Max, Gina is looking to buy a new car and as you know a bit about cars, I thought you could help. She doesn't want a little run-around, she wants something that looks and feels bigger but is still reasonable to run.'

Max was visibly irritated at this lame ploy to get him talking, particularly as his interest in cars was no more than the average man's. He'd have words with his sister later, but for now rather than cause a scene, he'd play along with their little game.

'You could try a Ford Escort or I've also heard the Honda Civic is quite a good buy.'

Gina caught Kate's eye and beckoned her over. Kate shook her head but Gina merely called. 'Kate, here a minute, darling.'

Kate gave her friend an accusatory look but walked over nonetheless.

'Kate, we were talking about my new car. Max has suggested either a Ford Escort or a Honda Civic, what do you think?'

What new car? This is the first I've heard about it, Kate thought to herself and then looked aghast, she knew nothing about cars and could really make herself look stupid in front of Max. Of all the daft conversations to start, why did Gina pick this one?

Her thoughts continued. As she pondered how to respond to this without showing herself up she saw Gina and Louise withdraw. She looked at Max,

'I think we've been set up. I'm sorry about my friend. Subtlety was never her strong suit.'

'Don't apologise. I think she was merely my sister's co-conspirator.'

They smiled awkwardly at each other and then an even more awkward silence fell between them. Just as Kate begun looking for an escape route Max added, 'That was delicious beef by the way. What was in the marinade?'

'Ginger, brown sugar and soy sauce. Just equal quantities of each and a little water,' Kate answered flirtatiously.

'Well, it was certainly very tasty. Do you like to cook?'

'I do, when I have someone to cook for, but I live alone and it's not much fun cooking for one...' she paused, cursing herself for being so apparent but continued. 'Although I do occasionally invite friends over for dinner, and sometimes my parents.'

Kate winced as her inane answer came tumbling out of her mouth. *Oh God! He's going to think I'm so sad and a babbling moron*, she thought to herself.

But he merely replied, 'I know the feeling well. I live alone too.'

After another short silence, which seemed to go on forever and in which they both looked everywhere but at each other, he asked, 'What do you do for a living?'

'I'm a teacher, at Middleton Comprehensive. I teach English'

'Remind me never to write to you, my spelling is atrocious.'

Kate laughed a little too heartily at such a weak joke. 'What do you do?' she added.

'I work in banking.'

'High Street or Merchant?'

Max was visibly taken aback at this informed question rather than the usual "give us a loan" type reply that he normally encountered.

'I work for a firm of Merchant bankers in London.'

'The commute must be tiring.'

'Not as tiring as spending all day with thirty teenagers.'

And from there on they quickly found an empathy and ease with one another. Max offered Kate another drink and suggested they sat down. Their conversation at once deepened into the more meaningful, and Kate answered Max's questions with a candour that surprised even her. Max made it clear that he was very family-orientated, he loved his sister, respected his father, adored his mother and his greatest wish was to be a father himself someday. When he asked Kate her views on having children, she answered,

'I'd love to be a Mum. I wouldn't have a child with just anyone but if I found the right man and our relationship was stable. I think that to become parents would be a natural progression.'

She surprised herself that she had admitted this much to a man she hardly knew, when she had only just admitted it to herself.

Their conversation continued along the same vein, neither of them feeling the need to hold back or play verbal volleyball, both at ease with total honesty. When they finally paused and looked around they realised they were two of the last there. Gina had said her goodbyes earlier and told Kate where she'd hide her key. Louise had also long gone. Max suggested they share a taxi, assuring her they were going in the same direction.

At Gina's house, Max declined any contribution for the taxi fare, took Kate's telephone number with a promise to call and said goodbye. Kate crept into Gina's house, shut the door quietly so as not to disturb her and was greeted with an enthusiastic 'Well, how did it go?'

Gina hadn't been able to sleep and so had got up and waited for her friend for a full post-mortem.

'Oh Gina, I've blown it! He didn't even try and give me a goodnight kiss.'

'Whoa…back a few paces please my girl and start at the beginning.'

Kate relayed the gist of the conversation about settling down and having children and ended, 'I've scared him off, haven't I?'

'Not necessarily,' Gina comforted. 'After all, he was just as open and as full on as you. He might just be a perfect gentleman, or shy. We do know he is quite shy, don't we?'

'I suppose so,' Kate conceded but she wasn't convinced and she wasn't sure Gina was either.

'Anyway,' Gina continued. 'We can't do anything more about it now so lets get some sleep and I'm sure things will look better in the morning.'

And with that the two friends went to bed.

Gina already had the coffee brewing when Kate emerged the next morning.

'Morning Kate, How are you feeling?'

'Stupid,' moaned Kate.

'Oh don't be so hard on yourself Kate, I don't think it's as bad as you think. Here, drink this,' Gina suggested as she handed Kate a coffee.

'I just wish I had your confidence, still I suppose you're right, there's nothing I can do about it now. I'll just have to wait and see if he calls and if he doesn't then he's not the man for me.'

Gina gave her friend a quizzical look, not really believing her ears. Was this really her Kate being so philosophical when in the past she'd have analysed every word and action *ad infinitum*?

'And another thing,' Kate continued. 'I'm not going to wait by the 'phone just in case he calls. If he 'phones while I'm out and he's serious then he'll try again until he gets me.'

'Hang on a minute. What's this U-turn all about? You sound as if you couldn't care less whether he calls you or not and I know that's not how you feel.'

'No it isn't, but I can't put my life on hold until a man makes it complete. I've got to find contentment alone, assume I will be on my own and then if I do find a soul mate, that will be a bonus.'

'What's got into you, Kate?' Gina interrupted. 'Only last night you were really excited at the prospect of finally meeting Max and now, only twelve hours on, you're planning a lifetime of solitude.'

'Oh Gina, I'm not explaining myself very well am I? I did, I do like Max and I'd really love for it to work out but I can't pin all my hopes for happiness on a man, whoever he is. I've got to live my life for me and not keep subjecting myself to emotional traumas that are out of my control. I'm not really being flippant…I suppose I'm just trying to protect myself.'

'Oh you silly cow,' Gina mocked affectionately. 'You can't fool me. I know you want Max to 'phone and I'm sure he will. But I agree with you about one thing. You can't sit waiting by the 'phone for him to call, so how about we get ready and find a nice country pub for Sunday lunch?'

'Great idea Gina, but I'll have to go home after lunch. Not to wait by the 'phone, but I've got a pile of end of year school reports to complete.'

'That suits me. I've got some housework to do before Joe brings Kieran home.'

*   *   *   *   *

Kate had been writing reports for three hours when she picked up the blank form for Jimmy Granger. She paused as she pondered this lad. She was supposed to be objective but Jimmy Granger gave 'obnoxious' a new definition. School reports had to focus on the positive and she was finding it difficult to think of something good to write about him. 'His school tie was always neatly knotted,' wouldn't really suffice.

Her thoughts were suddenly interrupted by the telephone ringing. She picked up the receiver expecting to reassure Gina that she was fine. Her heart missed a beat when the voice on the other end of the line answered, 'Hello Kate, it's me, Max.'

'Oh hello Max, how are you?'

'I'm fine, thanks, how are you? Are you busy?'

'Just writing school reports. Nothing that can't wait.'

'I was wondering if you would like to go out for dinner one evening?'

'I'd love to.'

'How about next Thursday?'

'That'll be fine, I've nothing planned.'

'I'll pick you up at about 7.30pm if that's okay?'

'Of course, I'll look forward to it.'

'See you Thursday then.'

'Okay Max, bye.'

'Bye Kate.'

Kate put down the receiver, gave a little squeal of delight and then dialled Gina's number.

'Hi Gina, it's me. He's 'phoned.'

'That's great news Kate. And…?'

'He asked me out for dinner next Thursday.'

'I take it you said yes.'

'Of course.'

Both friends chuckled, made arrangements to meet for lunch the following Friday and said their goodbyes.

Kate returned to her school reports, picked up the blank form and began to write. "Jimmy has a strong personality and always adds an interesting dimension to class discussions…"

*   *   *   *   *

Thursday was a long time coming although Kate didn't have a moment to spare. When she wasn't teaching or writing reports she was either on the telephone spreading her good news or sorting through her wardrobe for the perfect outfit. She had finally decided upon outfit number seven; a white dress with a bold print, a fitted bodice, full skirt and puff sleeves. The neckline was a low sweetheart and was a perfect combination of demure with a suggestion of vamp. Max arrived promptly at 7.30pm although Kate had been ready for an hour. When she opened the door for him her natural smile hid the analytical look in her eyes as she scoured his face intently for his reaction. He was obviously pleased to see her and approved of what he saw.

'Hi, would you like to come in for a minute?' she asked.

'I'd love to but I think we'd better go straight away as I've booked the table for eight.'

'Okay, I'll just get my bag and I'm ready.'

At that precise moment the phone rang. Kate looked at Max apologetically as she lifted the receiver to her ear.

'Hi Kate, it's me - Geoffrey,' came the very cheerful introduction. Kate's jaw dropped as he added, 'It didn't work out with Tracey and I've found myself thinking about you a lot recently.'

'Oh!' Kate replied curtly, irritated that after all this time he could be so arrogant as to presume that he could contact her again and even more irritated that he had chosen this particular moment in which to do it.

'Yes,' he continued. 'And I was wondering if we could meet up sometime for a drink?'

'What?' she asked incredulously, her eyes widening.

'Oh, I don't mean like that, I wouldn't expect anything like that, not after what I've put you through. I mean just as friends,' he added in his most conciliatory tone.

'*You* might need a friend,' Kate offered sternly. 'But I most certainly do *not*.' And with that she slammed down the receiver.

'Anyone important?' Max enquired lightly.

'No-one of any consequence,' she replied as she gave him one of her brightest smiles.

She shut her door and followed him to his car whereupon he opened the passenger door for her. *This man has class,* she thought to herself. *Knows how to treat a woman.*

As they drove to the restaurant they chatted about their respective working days, how beautiful the weather was and how it promised to be a hot summer. It was a short drive to the restaurant and Max had chosen a new, up-market establishment that even the worldly-wise Kate hadn't known about. Even if she had, she wouldn't have been there as it wasn't the kind of place you'd come to with a friend. Max offered Kate his arm and, as they walked in, Kate was immediately impressed. It had the ambience of a swish London restaurant but also the intimacy of a romantic bistro. They were ushered to a lounge area, offered an apéritif and given the menus to peruse.

Kate felt nervous; not the usual first date nerves but that indescribable stomach fluttering she hadn't experienced since she was a teenager on her first ever date. She had to admit to herself that she was smitten with Max, much more than she knew was good for her. After they had chosen their food, Max ordered a bottle of *Chateneuf Du Pape*, an impressive full-bodied red, with a price tag to match. Kate smiled inwardly at this clue. Max was trying to impress her as much as she was him. When their starters were ready they were invited to their table. Their conversation was light and easy as they exchanged their views and likes and dislikes about anything and everything.

Kate had just broken off a piece of bread roll, buttered it and popped it into her mouth when she dropped her hand and caught the end of her butter-knife. It started to somersault through the air, almost in slow motion, and landed at the feet of a neighbouring diner. Kate felt mortified, but the arrival of a waiter discreetly replacing her knife and removing the offending one from the floor gave her the moment she needed to compose herself. Max displayed a slight half-smile, but he was far too polite to comment. At that moment he had realised Kate was just as nervous as he was and that enabled him to relax. Kate relaxed also; she had done what she was dreading; made a fool of herself and so she hoped things couldn't get any worse. That was the case because the evening continued without further incident.

When he dropped her off at her home, he declined her invitation for a coffee as he had to be at work early the following day but suggested meeting again next week and made arrangements to pick her up at 7.30pm the following Wednesday. He then lunged forward, gave her a swift kiss on the cheek and disappeared into the night. Kate was left feeling disappointed that he had gone with only the ghost of his kiss on her cheek, but elated with the warm glow she felt inside.

The following day she met Gina for lunch and gave her a blow by blow account of the evening. They laughed at the butter-knife incident although Kate conceded you had to be there to appreciate the comedy. They also met that evening for their usual Friday night jaunt although Kate's heart wasn't in it and she was disappointed that they didn't spot Max out with his friends, as she'd secretly hoped for.

Max called for Kate as arranged the following Wednesday, and they went for a quiet drink at a country pub. They sat in the garden on this gloriously balmy summer's evening and chatted easily and effortlessly all night. When he dropped her off at home, he again declined her invitation for a coffee but this time he drew her to him and kissed her on the mouth. A long slow gentle kiss that left her open-mouthed and speechless as he left.

Two days later Kate and Gina were sitting at their usual table at their usual wine bar when Max and his friends arrived.

'Oh shit!' exclaimed Kate. 'I'm wearing the same dress I wore on our first date. He'll think I've got nothing else to wear.'

Gina laughed. 'As if he's worried about what you're wearing, you klutz! It's the present he's interested in, not the wrapping paper!' she mocked.

Max came over and after chatting politely to both women, asked if they'd mind breaking their tradition of going out together on a Friday night so he could take Kate out next week. He went on to explain that he found it difficult to go out for an evening, and then get up early the following day to catch a train for work. Gina answered for Kate, saying of course they didn't mind, their arrangement wasn't set in stone, and so Max and Kate made arrangements for the following Friday. He returned to his friends, finished his drink and left with them, rather too quickly for Kate's liking.

'What's up friend?' Gina quizzed.

'Oh, I don't know, he seems wonderful and keen when we're together but it's as though he doesn't want to spend too much time with me. It's going to be a whole week before we see each other again and since the barbecue I've only had two proper dates with him.'

Gina let out an exasperated sigh. 'He's just explained why he finds it difficult to see you mid-week.'

'I know,' Kate went on the defensive. 'But what's wrong with tomorrow. It's Saturday and he doesn't have to go to work on Sunday, does he?

'Don't worry,' Gina responded a little more patiently. 'He's definitely interested, he's probably got other commitments or doesn't want to rush things or, or I don't know but stop worrying, it'll be alright.'

'I suppose you're right, again. It's just that…'

'I know,' Gina interrupted. 'But stop torturing yourself, come on, drink up, let's move on.'

And with that the two girls continued their Friday night together.

CHAPTER 16

Claire and Richard announced their engagement in the local papers, having first told their closest friends of the big party they were hosting in their new home to celebrate. Claire had invited Gina plus a guest but Gina had decided to go alone as she was not intending to stay late and wanted her departure time to be in her own hands. The healing process required after Paul's deception was coming to an end but only after she had put her own needs first and taken time to come to terms with that particular chapter in her life.

She arrived by taxi – a treat reserved for special occasions – and felt apprehensive as she knocked on the door. Lively music was reverberating out of the open windows and lifted Gina's spirits instantly as she noticed that everything about the house looked and smelt brand new, right down to the garden ornaments and the welcome mat that she was standing on. She smiled, nodding her head in acknowledgement that, at last, Claire seemed to have everything, and Gina was delighted for her. Through the glass-stained window of the front door she could see Claire's outline coming towards her and she could hear the laughter of what seemed like hundreds of people.

'Gina, Gina, come in. I was getting worried about you,' Claire said excitedly, looking beautiful in a cream suit and with her raven black hair cut into a new bob showing off her enviable high cheekbones to perfection. She had always looked younger than her 30 years but now she was positively radiant. Gina hugged her friend and apologised for being late.

'I thought I would treat myself to a taxi but it was half an hour late. I'm so sorry. Are there many here?' she asked as she handed over her engagement gift while taking in the welcoming aura of the small but refined surroundings.

'You lucky cow Claire,' she continued without waiting for an answer. 'The most handsome man in Cambridge and a lovely home. You owe me mate!'

'Enough of that Gina, I've thanked you plenty for giving me a passage to Richard. I had something to do with it too you know! Anyway, some of his friends are not too bad either, as you'll see for yourself. There are a quite few here so, come on, let's get you a drink and back into circulation.'

Heads turned as Gina walked into the kitchen but she ignored the group of men in the corner who were nudging each other and smiling their best smiles in her direction. Gina loved being noticed. All her adult life she had felt that the only good thing about being a woman was the attention that it brought from the opposite sex and she had no compunction whatsoever about making the most of it. Mother Nature had given women a gift – the power to turn men into mush to compensate them for their lack of physical strength – and using it now and again was a given right, almost obligatory.

After pouring herself a glass of wine she turned to find herself face to face with one of the men who had been standing in the group, and his closeness made her jump.

'Sorry. I didn't mean to startle you. My name's Simon and I just had to tell you that your presence has brightened up what was a very dull day. And you are…?' he asked as he opened a can of beer, spraying some of its contents into Gina's face. He apologised immediately but made matters worse by flapping around for some kitchen towels and then trying to wipe her down as his friends looked on with expressions of disbelief. Gina had no intention of giving them the satisfaction of rejecting this poor man, who now looked as if he was quietly praying for an alien abduction.

'You don't waste much time in making an impact, do you?' she laughed as she finished mopping up the last of the beer from her face and neck. 'Hi, I'm

Gina and nice to meet you Simon,' she replied before taking a much-needed sip of her wine.

Although he was attractive in a boyish way, Simon did not appeal to her physically and she certainly didn't want to spend the whole evening being chatted up by him but for the moment she decided to enjoy his company, keeping it friendly with no flirting. After a few drinks he asked her if she wanted to go into the lounge, where everybody was dancing to sounds of the 70's, and she accepted. She loved to dance but only with the relaxing influence of some alcohol, without which the flailing of arms and the jerking of legs appeared to Gina to be the actions of a lunatic. The room was in full swing when she spotted the latest arrival to be greeted warmly by Richard, in the shape of a leather-clad male. Gina could not hear what they were saying to each other but continued to watch with interest catching only that his name was Matt. Simon tried to grab her hand but she smiled sweetly and danced away from him whilst her gaze remained transfixed. This did not deter her companion who continued to shuffle in front of her, heedless to the fact that her attention was elsewhere.

Matt took off his helmet to reveal short, sun-kissed blond hair and the most piercing blue eyes Gina had ever seen. She was captivated by this vision of manliness and her surroundings melted away as she watched him hug his friend and then turn to see who was in the room. Matt scanned the lounge until he spotted Gina, and their eyes locked. Gina decided to give him one of her dazzling smiles but he just stared back intently with a gleam in his eyes that conveyed all. Her heart raced wildly and her cheeks flushed with excitement, as in that one fleeting moment she knew that he would come to her. All she had to do was wait.

The lights had been dimmed and the music turned up when Simon asked Gina if she wanted to rest. She said she would for a while and after they sat down in one corner of the room, he started to tell her his life story. It soon became evident that she had landed herself with the party bore, or at the very least a strong contender – pleasant enough but whose favourite subject was himself, his job and his money. As he talked he would often look around or stare just past Gina's head, as if he was hoping for a wider audience. She knew he was trying to impress her but little did he know that there was nothing in his power to change a thing. Her mind was somewhere else now as she wondered how long it would be before Matt approached her and how she was going to free herself kindly from Simon. At that moment Matt walked into the room and appeared to be searching for someone. Gina pretended not to be looking but knew that this was the moment of truth. Just as she was about to politely take her leave, Simon announced that he needed the little boy's room and would be back in no time.

'Don't go away now, will you? I haven't told you the best bit yet,' he insisted as he rose unsteadily onto his feet as his demolition of several cans of beer was beginning to take its toll.

Best bit of what? Gina thought, having almost lost the will to live listening about his antics on his last holiday to the Caribbean.

'Oh, don't worry. I'm not going anywhere,' she said honestly, because now she could see that Matt was hovering nearby and, wasting no time at all, appeared in front of her but not before converging with the departing Simon. The temptation to laugh was too much for Gina so she bent her head downwards and put her hand to her mouth in an attempt to stifle a giggle.

'What's so funny?' Matt asked as he handed her a fresh glass of wine while searching her face for a clue to the joke and continued with a smile. 'I think I can guess. Let's just say I'm not known for my patience and that guy has hardly let you out of his sight. Now it's my turn and Gina, I won't be making the same mistake as him.'

Gina didn't ask how he knew her name. That was obvious and she was flattered that he had gone out of his way to find out. At that moment she was concentrating on pretending not to be nervous because this guy was surely the most attractive man she had ever spoken to. In fact, if she didn't know better, she would think that she had just fallen in love at first sight.

'Actually, I've been waiting for you,' Gina smiled back unable to help her candour. It came naturally to her but she immediately regretted not playing it a bit cooler. 'I mean, I knew you would come and that all I had to do was…' she trailed off as she watched him smile a knowing smile, which made them both erupt into laughter. Simon walked back into the room, and looking unimpressed, muttered something incoherent in Matt's ear, before walking away in disgust. Gina rose from her seat to go after him and explain that it was nothing personal but Matt shrugged his shoulders and took her in his arms for a slow dance.

Gina didn't resist and nuzzled up to his neck feeling comfortable, safe and exhilarated. His natural smell was intoxicating and as their bodies moved closer, the lights were dimmed some more as if just for them, and Gina hoped the night would never end.

*   *   *   *   *

Kate didn't have much time to fret about her situation as it was the last week of term and her work schedule was frantic as she tried to get everything completed before the long summer vacation. She did, however, resolve to talk to Max about it when they met, to find out how exactly he felt about her. She didn't want to scare him off but she had to know where she stood. With the long summer vacation ahead of her she'd have too much time to think and she didn't want to spend it in an emotional limbo.

That Friday Max arrived promptly as usual and suggested the cinema. They went to see a romantic adventure and were both lost in the film. Afterwards Max asked Kate what she would like to do and she suggested coffee at her house. Max accepted. They were both sipping their coffee when Max asked,

'Are you OK? You seem quieter than usual.'

Kate realised this was her opportunity and grasped the mettle.

'Well, you don't really know what is usual for me, do you?' she asked, smiling half-heartedly.

'I suppose I don't, but I'd like to.'

Kate was surprised at Max's reply, she had been expecting to make a few more caustic comments to get him to open up but his candour threw her off guard.

'If that's true then why do you only want to see me once a week?'

'Because I'm frightened.'

Kate looked at him nonplussed and waited for more.

'I've never felt like this about anybody so quickly before, and it scares me,' Max added.

'I feel the same,' Kate replied. 'But why are you scared?'

'I'm scared of getting hurt.'

'And you think I'll hurt you?'

'That's just it, I don't know. As you've just said yourself, I don't know you very well, do I?'

Kate beamed at him with genuine affection in her eyes. 'Oh! Max, I've been going round and round in circles trying to figure out whether you liked me or couldn't care less and I've been trying to convince myself that I'm not bothered either way. But I am. I really do like you. I can't promise you that either of us won't get hurt because who knows how things will work out. All I know is I want to get to know you better and the last thing I want to do is hurt you, quite the opposite actually.' She smiled at him again.

They looked at each other in silence for a while.

'Can I suggest something?' she added.

'Go on,' he encouraged.

'That we start again. We're both too long in the tooth to play games. Let's just let things go at their own pace.'

'Agreed,' he chuckled.

Kate made more coffee and they chatted easily for some time before Max finally said, 'I suppose I'd better be making a move.'

'You don't have to,' replied Kate coyly.

'I know, and I don't really want to but I think I'd better, before I do something I'll regret.'

'And would you regret it?'

'Let's not get into any more analysing tonight. I just feel I should go. But don't read anything else into it, okay? I'll call you tomorrow and perhaps we can get together on Sunday.'

She was about to argue her point when Max drew her to him and kissed her passionately. It was a long lingering kiss and it melted away all Kate's resistance.

Finally he pulled away and said hoarsely, 'I really had better go. I'll speak to you tomorrow.'

Kate smiled sweetly, 'I'll look forward to it.'

She rose with him and accompanied him to the door. He kissed her again. 'Bye,' he said.

'Bye,' she replied.

*   *   *   *   *

Gina sat in front of her dressing table mirror, staring solemnly at the naked face reflecting back. It was a strange moment where she felt that her body seemed to be outside of itself, looking down on her whole life. She took off the towel that was wrapped around her head and proceeded to comb through her wet hair. Still feeling confused she continued to look deep into her own eyes, almost trance-like, until her body gave way to an uncontrollable shiver, as if someone had walked over her grave. 'What's the matter Gina? What are you trying to tell yourself?' she asked as she gently untangled her hair, allowing the curls to fall back into their natural position. There was nothing obvious that came to mind so deciding that it was nothing more sinister than just nerves, and some anxiety about meeting Matt's sister and brother-in-law that evening, she pushed her confusion to one side reaching out to press the button on her radio. The local news was on, relaying the details of a nasty, tragic accident that had happened in the town killing two young boys who had been joy-riding. She shivered again and, annoyed at herself for momentarily getting her priorities wrong, gave herself a good talking to.

'So pull yourself together girl. His family are just human beings like you and there's nothing to worry about,' she continued loudly as she pointed a finger at her reflection.

Gina's thoughts then switched to the way the relationship with Matt was progressing. He was loving, attentive and made her feel as if she was the loveliest creature he had ever known. In return, over the last few weeks, she had dropped her barriers and had given herself to him in a way she had never done before, not even with Joe. She now understood the meaning of the word 'soul-mate' and her trust in Matt was so complete that life was once again fulfilling and luxurious. They had both decided it was time to meet each other's family, starting with his sister Leanne and her husband Ross, then their respective parents, and finally Kieran. But before that she would start dropping Matt's name into conversations with Kieran to let him know sensitively that there was somebody special on the scene. Her heart missed a beat and the horrible butterflies were back in her stomach. Perhaps that was why she was feeling so strange – the thought of Kieran not liking Matt? No impossible, who could fail to love Matt? He was just adorable. What if Matt didn't like Kieran? Again, unthinkable. Gina smiled. He was even more adorable! Yes that must be it. Worrying about nothing at all, silly girl.

An hour later, Gina was ready and this time, when she looked in the mirror, there was no apprehension, just a delicious anticipation of the evening ahead.

Matt picked her up and drove her to his sister's house, a beautiful, imposing Regency affair set in a quaint village in West Suffolk.

'Wow, Matt!' Gina clapped her hands together with glee. 'Please tell me that your parents buy all their offspring a house like this when they get married,' she said mischievously, not caring if it sounded too presumptuous.

'I wish. Are you hinting again young lady?' he smiled as he playfully pushed the tip of her nose with his finger. Matt did this often; as he loved her small, turned up nose with its summertime freckles.

'Certainly not,' Gina replied, flicking her hair back dramatically as she squeezed his bottom.

'Behave. My sister's now walking down the hallway.'

Leanne opened the door to reveal a huge reception area. 'Come in. It's lovely to meet you, Gina,' she said politely as she shook Gina's hand and then gave her younger brother a loving hug.

Matt led Gina into the kitchen and introduced her to his brother-in-law.

'This is Ross and you need to watch him. In fact there should be a government health warning round this guys neck.'

Gina gave Matt one of her 'where are you taking me with this?' looks as he continued. 'He's the funniest guy I've ever known and I guarantee that your jaw will ache by the end of night – you'll be begging for him to stop!'

And so it was. Ross was hilarious the whole time and Gina thought he was even funnier than Billy Connelly, her favourite comedian. Although slightly overweight and balding, he had strong features with long eyelashes protecting pale blue eyes and he became more attractive as the hours went by. Leanne had an unusual, exotic beauty with long chestnut hair reaching down to her waist, almond shaped eyes, a long straight nose and a generous mouth.

Leanne and Gina chatted endlessly, pausing only to top up their glasses or to clear away the table in readiness for the next course. Gina insisted on helping Leanne to wash the dishes and clean the kitchen as they continued to laugh and gossip while the men smoked cigars over a glass of port. They discovered much about each other as the evening progressed, sharing small secrets and their love for Matt, with unashamed pride. The warmth and kindness of both hosts struck Gina as she acknowledged that she had never felt more at home, outside of her own family, in all of her years.

Matt did not take his eyes off Gina the whole evening and loved the way her eyes sparkled as she laughed at Ross' jokes and the fact that she had so quickly felt comfortable in his family's company. It was one of the best evenings that either could remember for some time and, after thanking Ross and Leanne several times for the wonderful food, they headed off down the long pathway, hand in hand.

'I think I'd better buy a hat!' Leanne whispered to Ross as they stood at the front door, waving goodbye to their guests.

*   *   *   *   *

Kate was lying in bed, smiling inwardly as she wallowed in the luxury of the first day of her six weeks of leisure, when the telephone rang. She reached across and grabbed the receiver from the bedside extension.

'Good morning Kate.'

'Good morning Max, this is a surprise.' Kate sat up, fluffing up her hair and wiping the sleep from her eyes.

'A pleasant one I hope?'

'Of course,' she smiled fluttering her eyelashes.

There was a short pause before he continued in a serious tone. 'I want to explain about last night.'

Kate swung her feet to the floor and threw her duvet to one side. 'Go on,' she invited.

'I was just being foolish. Anyway, I don't really want to wait until tomorrow to see you again. Are you doing anything today?' he asked hopefully.

'I haven't made any plans.'

'Do you fancy spending the day together?' he added quickly.

'That would be lovely.'

'Great. How about I come round in an hour?'

Kate caught a glimpse of herself in her bedroom mirror and pulled a face. 'Better make it two,' she replied and then added quickly, 'I'm still in bed.'

'Oh, I'm sorry, did I wake you?'

'No, don't be silly. I was just being lazy. See you in a couple of hours. Bye.'

Kate leapt off the bed, made herself a coffee and then quickly tidied her house before having a bath, putting on her make-up, styling her hair and dressing in a pair of jeans and a crisp white shirt. She had only just finished when the doorbell rang, although her calm demeanour as she opened the door belied the frantic activity of the previous two hours.

Max swept her unto his arms and kissed her tenderly. 'I've been wanting to do this all morning.'

He kissed her again and then asked, 'Ready to go?'

'Yes, absolutely. I don't know what you've planned for today but I am a bit peckish,' a flushed Kate replied.

'Okay, so let's make the first stop lunch and we'll take it from there.'

The day that followed was truly wonderful and was akin to the best romantic movies: a collage of intimate interludes with the searing music being the only missing element. A walk through the picturesque countryside was followed by a light lunch at a country pub, a boat trip along a tranquil river and then a cream-tea at a remote English tea-room. Finally a drive to the coast to play in the amusement arcade was rounded off with a fish and chip supper out of the paper as they walked along the promenade. The entire day was punctuated with endless conversation and physical demonstrations of affection.

Back at Kate's house they reflected on their glorious day together over coffee. They fell silent and for a split second they both tensed before Max took hold of Kate and kissed her passionately.

'I want you so much.' His voice was hoarse with desire.

'Oh Max,' she started to respond but he muffled her with his kisses.

The emotions inside them, which they had both been suppressing, finally erupted and they fell into a passionate embrace. They both knew what was going to happen but neither rushed in. This wasn't mere lust taking over, this was the beginning of something deeper, more significant and both of them instinctively knew tonight was going to be special. Neither of them wanted to sully the memory of this night by acting impatiently and so without speaking they both pulled away. They kissed and touched and caressed for the longest time before Max took Kate's hand and led her upstairs. They helped each other undress and got into bed, all the time kissing and touching. They were gentle and considerate with one another as if savouring every moment. Their caresses slowly became more ardent and their passion became more intense until Max huskily spoke.

'Oh Kate, I need you so much.'

She kissed him fervently and he moved to cover her, slowly and gently entering her. They began to rock in unison, very gently at first but gradually increasing in tempo until their mutual passion finally took over and they were locked together as though they were one entity. They moved together more fervently constantly seeking out each other's mouths until the core of their passions slowly erupted within them and climaxed in unison as their bodies convulsed together in a glorious crescendo. They lay together kissing and stroking one another, without the need for words and finally fell asleep in one another's arms, completely sated and in love.

*   *   *   *   *

Gina had been surprised to receive a call that morning from Leanne asking if she fancied getting together for a coffee. She had accepted warmly, flattered that the invitation had come so soon after their first meeting. Gina hurried towards the coffee shop where they had agreed to meet and felt nervous but excited at the prospect of seeing this lovely lady again. She had been worried for most of the morning and several times had told herself not to be so stupid. After all, the evening had been wonderful and everyone had enjoyed each other's company. So what was there to feel anxious about? But being on a one to one with someone as important as Matt's sister was not so easy without the support and comfort of others around her. As Gina opened the door of the coffee shop, she did what was almost an automatic reaction in a situation like this; she lifted her face and ordered her body to take on its most confident language, one that spoke of being in control and totally comfortable with it's owner. She spotted Leanne in the corner perusing the menu and, through the bustle and noise, made her way towards her. Leanne beamed up at her.

'Hi Gina. I hope you don't mind but I've already ordered the coffees. It's difficult to get served in here when it's as busy as this. By the way are you eating?'

Gina hesitated as she could not afford the luxury of eating in cafés and had brought in a packed lunch, but not wanting to leave Leanne to eat on her own decided to sit on the fence. 'I'll eat if you are. I really don't mind either way,' she replied as she glanced at the menu in front of her while taking off her jacket and laying it out on the back of the chair.

'In that case I'd rather not. The prices are a bit steep don't you think?

Gina nodded, relieved at this decision after spotting the price for a jacket potato with baked beans and cheese. 'I'd rather go hungry actually Leanne,' she laughed. 'At these prices I could put down a deposit on my own restaurant.'

At this point the coffees arrived and silence fell between them. They both went to speak at the same time.

'No, you first,' Gina insisted as she poured sugar into her soup-like bowl of cappuccino.

'I was just going to say that I really enjoyed the other evening and that I'm so pleased that Matt has finally found himself a gorgeous woman like you. And I don't just mean on the outside.'

Gina was totally taken aback and nearly choked on her drink. 'Really?' was all she could muster as a reply while a big smile emerged across her face, despite her attempts to try to hide her delight.

'Yes, really,' Leanne was amused but continued. 'I've never seen him so in love but don't tell him I told you so, will you?'

Gina shook her head. 'As if I would,' she replied and added 'Well, welcome to the Mutual Appreciation Society because I was just thinking the same about you. And Ross of course.'

'I'll have to tell him that. He's not often described as gorgeous. Except by me, of course!'

Leanne went on to say that she thought Gina would be around for a long time to come and wanted them to become good friends.

'Nothing would please me more,' Gina replied as she held up her cup to toast their new friendship.

CHAPTER 17

That summer had been perfect. In the long hot days and weeks of the summer vacation Kate and Max had spent more and more time together and very quickly forgot what life was like without the other. Kate took Max to meet her parents, he took her to meet his and they also visited Sandie and David in Surrey. All these momentous occasions went very well and Kate thought that she would burst with happiness. As Gina was also experiencing the same with Matt, it made it possible for her to exude such happiness without compunction. When the friends got together they exchanged their romantic gossip like a pair of over-excited giggling teenagers and revelled not only in their own, but also in each other's joy.

Kate thought life couldn't get any more perfect, but it did. When she returned to school in the September, Howard was a changed man. He was charming and friendly and the perfect boss. Kate assumed that he must have thought long and hard over the summer about the events of last term, and had decided to call a truce. So her professional life, now as good as her personal life, was the icing on her cake.

This assumption, however, was a little premature. The first time he touched her arm, as they laughed at a joke, she hardly noticed. Nor the second time when he placed both hands on her shoulders as he squeezed past her in the English storeroom. Nor the third, nor the fourth. When she stiffened at his fifth 'matey' hug, he apologised for overstepping the mark but Kate thought she spotted a slight smirk around his mouth. She glared at him the next time and he responded by holding out his hands palms upwards, and enquiring with mock innocence 'What?' It soon became obvious to Kate that Howard was trying a new ploy. He was disguising his advances as friendly touches and if she objected he would merely infer that it was her paranoia that was making her over-react. And for a while she tried to convince herself that this was indeed the case, because she didn't want to believe the alternative. But when the touches became a brush against her breast or a pat on the buttock, she knew she wasn't mistaken. She also knew that she would have to confront him before too long, even though she feared it could mean losing her job.

Max arrived at 7pm, as arranged, and Kate had the meal ready. Over dinner she told him the whole Howard saga and the current dilemma she faced. Max got all macho and offered to "have it out with him" but Kate assured him that she could handle this herself as long as she could rely upon him for support. He responded that that went without saying. Kate immediately felt rather foolish. How could she have ever doubted that Max would be anything other than totally supportive? He even went so far as to suggest possible contingency plans should she find herself unemployed, although he stressed this was highly unlikely in view of the current employment legislation. Once they had exhausted the subject and Kate was happy once more, they relaxed and enjoyed their evening together. They went to bed promptly that night as Max had to get up early to catch his train to London.

When Max woke the following morning to find he had overslept, his heart sunk. His plans were in danger of being thwarted but, as he couldn't bear to delay them any longer, he resolved to go ahead with them just the same. He carefully laid a breakfast setting at the table, then poured orange juice into a glass, cereal into a bowl and the milk into a small jug beside it so that the cereal wouldn't get soggy. He popped bread into the toaster ready for toasting and coffee into a cafetierre ready for the boiling water. He then hurried into the bathroom for a quick shave and shower. Once out he started to dress and realising he was in danger of missing his train, he grabbed his jacket, coat, tie and cufflinks to put on later, along with his briefcase. As he left he carefully placed a small jewellery box in the centre of the breakfast table. As the front door slammed shut Kate thought she heard him mutter a few expletives. *He's late again*, Kate thought as she smiled inwardly to herself before turning over for just a few more minutes under the duvet.

Max threw everything he was carrying onto the passenger seat of his car and drove to the station in a state of panic. He parked the car, thanking whoever it was up there who had given him the foresight to buy a parking season ticket, grabbed his belongings from the passenger seat and ran to the station. He flashed his train ticket at the attendant, ran onto the platform and jumped onto the train as the guard slammed shut the door and blew his whistle. Max collapsed exhausted onto the nearest seat and, despite the painful stitch in his side, smiled at himself. He'd done it.

Kate had been lying in bed contemplating whether she should phone work and say she was ill. This was little more than half-hearted musing as her conscience wouldn't allow her to do this and so she reluctantly got up and headed downstairs. She beamed at the sight of her breakfast and let out a small sigh before going into the kitchen where she made her toast and coffee, carrying them back to the table. It was only when she sat down that she noticed the jewellery box placed carefully in front of her orange juice.

Once the feeling of satisfaction had sunk in and he had caught his breath, Max began to complete his dressing. He finally knotted his tie successfully on the third attempt, it being difficult without a mirror. He then folded back his shirt cuffs and opened his cufflink box at precisely the same moment as Kate opened the jewellery box in front of her.

Oh, the poor darling, Kate thought. *He's forgotten his cufflinks. Oh well, he'll just have to fold back his sleeves.*

'Oh! Shit, Fuck, Balls!' exclaimed Max as he stood up abruptly.

Everyone in the entire carriage seemed to fold down their newspapers simultaneously and glare at him in unified disgust. Max held up the engagement ring in the box and pointed to it by way of an explanation. One commuter peered disdainfully at him over the rim of his glasses.

'It's…wrong box…Kate…my cufflinks…Oh no…'

He sat back down in his seat, mute with despair and shook his head slowly and dejectedly. Slowly, one by one, the other passengers returned to their newspapers. One young female passenger gave him a weak half smile full of pity and sympathy.

That evening Max drove round to Kate's house immediately after getting off the train. She was surprised to see him as she was supposed to be going over to his house later on.

'What are you doing here? Not that I'm not pleased to see you, of course,' Kate reassured him and then added, 'Are you okay? You look a bit… odd.'

'Yeah, I'm fine. This morning… did you find a box?'

'Oh yes, your cufflinks, they're in my handbag. I was going to bring them round with me this evening. There was no need to come and pick them up.'

'No…um…er…I didn't mean to leave *them*. I meant to leave you this,' he explained as he thrust the box awkwardly towards her.

Kate took the box, opened it and stared at it in open-mouthed amazement. 'It's an engagement ring,'

'Said with all the detective cunning of Hercule Poirot. Yes, of course it is,' Max answered, as if there was some doubt as to what it was. 'I was hoping to do something spectacularly romantic, but it all went wrong. I suppose I'm just not cut out to be a romantic hero,' he sighed.

Kate's eyes were transfixed on the ring and after a pause he asked 'Well?'

'Well what?' Kate countered.

'Are you being deliberately dense?' Max exclaimed with some frustration. 'Will you marry me?'

'Not if you talk to me in that tone,' she joked with a broad smile on her face. Max looked hurt. 'Of course I will. There's nothing I want more than to be your wife,' she declared as she flung her arms around his neck and kissed him repeatedly.

*   *   *   *   *

Matt was being extremely secretive about Gina's birthday, insisting that she should wait for the evening before he disclosed where he intended to take her.

'But I don't know what to wear,' she had pleaded with him over the phone.

'And I've already told you that you can wear what you like. It's not my fault that you won't believe me.'

After a few silent moments he added mischievously, ' Oh, okay then.'

'What, you'll tell me where we're going?' she squealed with delight.

'No, I'll tell you what to wear!' he laughed as Gina muttered an expletive.

'Go on then. Do tell,' she replied with a sulky voice.

'That lovely, red dress that you wore when we had our first date. Pick you up at 7pm and don't be late.'

Kieran answered the door to Matt, throwing himself into his arms and shouting out proudly, 'Mummy's nearly ready and she looks beoooooutiful. And she's wearing the badge I made her at school.'

Gina walked through from the kitchen wearing the low-necked red dress that Matt had suggested and a big white round cardboard badge which had "The best mum is 31" handwritten in black with gold glitter on the edges.

'Isn't it lovely?' she asked Matt giving him a look that demanded total agreement or else.

'Absolutely. Not sure I'm going to be able to beat that one, Kieran,' Matt smiled as he put him down onto an armchair.

'Kate's upstairs so we can go now if you want,' Gina said eagerly.

Matt nodded so Gina hugged Kieran, being careful not to squash the badge which would result in hundreds of tiny glitter grains escaping onto his pyjamas, and shouted up the stairs 'Thanks Kate. Back before midnight.'

'Have a good time you two,' Kate replied as she emerged down the stairs. 'Come on then Kieran, lets read you a book before you go to bed.'

Gina was excited. Never before had anyone taken her to a surprise venue and she didn't care where it was as long as she was with Matt.

First he took her to a huge manor, set in beautiful Suffolk countryside, where a horse and cart were ready to take them to one of the oldest pubs in Britain. After a couple of drinks they returned to the manor, using the same mode of transport, where a beautiful dining room had been reserved for just the two of them. The waitress brought them a sumptuous four-course meal with champagne, coffee and liqueurs and when they were finished a three-man acappella group serenaded the birthday girl.

This was all too much for Gina and she could not stop the tears from welling up. As the beautiful voices continued to reverberate around the room, Matt suddenly went down on one knee and offered a small box to Gina who looked completely stunned. The music stopped and the waitress beckoned other waitresses from adjacent rooms to come and join them.

'Gorgeous, dazzling, wonderful Gina. Will you please do me the honour of becoming my wife?' he asked nervously, aware that he risked looking a complete fool in front of all these people. He closed his eyes momentarily, not daring to look up, and inwardly prayed for her positive answer. His anxiety was short-lived, however, for Gina shouted, 'Yes yes yes!' at the top of her voice and, as he opened his eyes wide to take in the scene, she gave him the biggest smile, kiss and hug she had ever given anyone in public. To a rapturous applause the couple sealed their future with a lingering passionate kiss.

CHAPTER 18

As Gina turned up the radio and continued to scrub the kitchen floor, she thought back to when Matt first broke the news that he and his four best friends had already booked a week's holiday before he had met her, and she smiled. He had looked so sheepish about his so-called big confession but Gina did not have a problem with it at all, even though she was going to miss him terribly. Once he had secured her blessing she could see that he was very excited about it and couldn't wait to hit the open roads on his motorbike. And now the holiday was imminent and she had promised him that she would prepare a special evening meal before he went away tomorrow.

She planned to finish the housework in double quick time so that she could concentrate on preparing one of her tastiest dishes. As her best friend Kate was convinced that it was her competent cooking that had impressed Max, perhaps there was something in this "through his stomach" malarkey, after all. Worth a try anyway. Roast beef, Yorkshire pudding and the crispiest of roast potatoes were on offer, followed by a home-made apple crumble and custard for desert. Not that she needed to find a way to her man's heart. They were engaged to be married and had decided that on his return from holiday they would move in together. They had also discussed the possibility of starting a family of their own, when the time was right. Gina had no misgivings about this and knew that Kieran would love to have a brother or sister. The rest of the day flew by as Gina prepared the house, dinner and herself so that everything was just perfect.

Matt arrived promptly at 7.30pm with a huge bunch of flowers, a bottle of champagne and wearing a sexy grin. Gina was thrilled to be treated this way. He never failed to make her heart beat wildly with anticipation.

'Roses and champers for my beautiful fiancée,' he whispered in her ear before kissing her neck and shoulders. 'God, you look gorgeous. And I'm very hungry.'

'Well not long to wait now,' she giggled extracting herself. 'Dinner will be ready in about half an hour.'

'I'm not talking about the dinner,' he grinned again, taking her hand to lead her up the stairs. 'That can wait.'

'But...'

The rest of her protest melted away when he took her in his arms and kissed her passionately. She waved a hand towards the kitchen but he continued to kiss her face, eyelids and neck while slowly pulling down the straps of her dress which fell to the floor. His eyes lit up at the absence of any underwear and as she stood there naked at the bottom of the stairs he pulled her closely to him and kissed her shoulders, working his way down around her breasts, lingering on her now swollen nipples. The cooking was forgotten as Gina quivered with expectancy and rested her hands around his shoulders pushing him down towards her stomach. He eagerly obliged, impatient to taste the sweetness of her womanhood and the juices of her desire. As his tongue explored deep into her, searching every part of her clitoris, she lost herself in the sheer ecstasy of his tender lovemaking.

'You're just so beautiful,' he murmured as he stopped to gaze at her body. 'And I love you so much'.

Gina drew him towards her so that she could meet his gaze. 'How much?' She asked, undoing the zip of his jeans.

'Oh let me see,' he replied thoughtfully, as Gina continued to take off his clothes. 'I know. More than all the twinkly bits in all the stars that have ever been in the sky.'

'Not much then,' she teased as she gently nibbled his ear.

Matt pulled her down to the floor of the lounge ensuring that all obstacles were not in their vicinity. The ensuing lovemaking was urgent and insatiable with the background music being drowned out by the collateral sounds of ecstasy. When their passions had been satisfied, they lay curled together for several minutes just listening to each other's breathing. Gina was the first to move, grabbing her clothes and making her way back to the kitchen.

'And still time for me to put in the Yorkshire puddings!' she joked.

After the meal they sat together listening to music, drinking wine and putting the world to rights. There had been no interruptions from anybody and the evening had been perfect. When they agreed it was time for bed Gina's face became grave and she informed Matt that there was one more thing he had to know about her before they finally got married.

'I can't go on with you not knowing the real me,' she said to him gently, by which time Matt looked concerned and could only muster an 'Oh, so what's that?'

'Just wait here and I'll show you.'

She left him sitting in confusion as she made her way up the stairs returning after 5 minutes.

'There!' She announced standing upright before him with her face staring straight ahead to avoid eye contact. 'So what do you think?'

'What do you mean, what do I think? What is it that you're showing me?' he replied, more confused than ever.

'Oh you're just being nice. Surely you can see the difference?' she said with a questioning expression and then continued. 'I decided that it was time for you see me without my make up on – barefaced, anaemic-looking, the real ugly me,' and then she crossed her arms as if to defy him to disagree.

'Gina, oh my special sweet Gina,' he replied, rising from the sofa and taking her into his reassuring arms. ' You had me worried there for a moment. Believe me when I say that you look even more beautiful without all that stuff over your face. Ugly indeed! Come on, let's go to bed. I don't know about you but I'm still hungry!'

*   *   *   *   *

Gina was counting the days, hours and minutes before Matt returned from his holiday. He had phoned her every day to let her know where he was and that he was having a great time but missing her madly. He had promised her he would never leave her again and that from now on any future holidays would include all three of them. Gina had also taken a week off from work and, while Kieran was at school, had caught up on her studies. This gave her the opportunity to ensure that she was always around for his phone calls. However, she had not heard from him since lunchtime the previous day and jumped up every time the phone rang. She cursed the many sales calls before settling back down to her coursework.

She was just relaxing after eating lunch when there was a knock at the door. Putting out a cigarette in the overflowing ashtray, she peered out of the window to see who it was. Leanne and Ross were standing at her front door looking pale and almost motionless. Gina was momentarily frozen to the spot and a feeling of utter dread just swept down her body, turning her legs into jelly. That familiar shiver, evident in recent weeks, returned violently taking over her whole body and, at that moment, she wanted to do anything in the world but open up her front door. Slowly she walked down the hallway and

140

took a deep breath before turning the latch. As she faced Ross, who now had a protective arm around Leanne, she could only croak, 'What's wrong?'

Without saying a word they entered the house and waited for the world to be shut away from their sight before they looked at her. Leanne spoke first. 'You'd better sit down, Gina. I have some terrible news.'

CHAPTER 19

Kate and Max sat opposite each other at a table for two in an intimate corner of Malone's, an out of town restaurant that specialises in good honest no-nonsense food.

'I always thought I'd like to get married on the beach of a tropical island somewhere, in a simple white column dress and bare feet, with a gentle breeze blowing my hair attractively off my face, and holding a single, white long-stemmed peace lily,' Kate mused, and before Max could respond, she added, 'But now it looks like becoming a reality I think I'd rather have a more traditional wedding.'

'I'm glad to hear it,' Max smiled with relief and then asked indulgently, 'and what exactly did you have in mind for this traditional wedding of yours?'

'Of ours,' Kate corrected in her best school marms' voice. 'Well I'd like a proper church wedding service at somewhere like the cathedral or the university chapel and then a reception in a marquee in the grounds of a stately home, or some castle or abbey ruins, or on the grassy banks of a river. And we'd have black bow-tied waiters serving a wedding breakfast of whole-poached salmons and tiger-prawn rings with exotic salads, baby new Jersey potatoes and then strawberries and cream with Pimms No.1. We'd then dance all evening to a live jazz and blues band and I think it had better be on a river bank so we could leave by boat with all our guests cheering and waving goodbye and...'

Max started to choke and a concerned Kate stopped mid-sentence as she immediately rose to offer assistance assuming a piece of his steak and kidney pudding was the cause.

Max put up his hand. 'I'm okay,' he said. 'I'm not choking on the food, just the thought of paying for all that lot,' he chastised with a twinkle in his eye.

'Oh!' responded a chagrined Kate. 'I suppose it is a tad extravagant,' she grinned.

'Just a tad,' replied Max with only the merest hint of sarcasm.

Kate pretended a hurt expression.

'Look Darling,' said Max softly as he sipped his wine. 'I don't mean to pour cold water over your ideas but we don't have unlimited funds and we really don't want to start married life up to our eyes in debt, do we? You know I'd do this for you if I could, don't you?'

'Yes, I know,' agreed Kate reluctantly. 'A girl just likes to dream, that's all.'

'Anyway,' Max interrupted quickly. 'It will all depend on what we can get at such short notice.'

'What do you mean?' quizzed Kate as she leant out of the way to allow the waiter to remove her plate.

'Well, I thought it would be nice to get married on Valentines Day.'

Kate's jaw dropped. 'What, February 14th?'

'That's what date Valentines Day usually falls on,' Max teased.

'Next year?' Kate queried incredulously.

'Yes,' reiterated Max as he tilted back on his chair enjoying Kate's reaction.

'But that's only about three months away.'

'Yes, I know. Which is why we'd better get a move on, don't you agree?'

'Of course I do,' beamed Kate. 'So what sort of wedding do you want then?'

'Pretty much as you described but just toned down a bit. You know, a church instead of a cathedral, a hotel banqueting room rather than a marquee and perhaps a disco instead of a live band.'

Kate paused for just a moment. 'That would be perfect,' she beamed.

'And another thing. Don't you think it's about time we moved in together and put one of the houses up for sale?' Max asked as topped up the wineglasses and looked at her expectantly.

'I must admit, I've been thinking the same. It seems silly paying two lots of bills when one house is nearly always unoccupied. Seeing as your house is nearer to the school and the railway station, it would be more practical for me to move in with you. What do you think?' Kate asked, raising her eyebrows to invite agreement.

'I thought the very same thing but didn't dare presume,' he ventured as he leant back, narrowly missing her playful swipe across his upper arm and added 'Well, let's eat up and get home for an early night. We've got a long day ahead of us tomorrow.'

'Why? What are we doing?'

'We're booking a wedding of course.'

*   *   *   *   *

The Excelsior Hotel had a wonderful faded elegance about it that Kate adored. The hotel had been built in the 1930's and was awash with original art deco features and decorations that reminded Kate of a far more refined age, one in which she would have loved to have lived. As she and Max sipped their coffee in the spectacular lobby she whispered 'I hope they can fit us in here, this place is just perfect.'

'Don't get your hopes up just yet darling, both Sunbury Hall and Clifton Court were fully booked and this might well be the same,' replied Max.

'I know, but having seen this place I'm so glad the other two were already booked up. This is better than both of them put together,' and then added hopefully, 'Anyway, it might be fate that they were both booked, it might be that someone up there watching over us knew we'd like this one more, or it might just be third time lucky.'

Max changed the subject tactfully. 'It was very good of the vicar to see us straight away. I thought the most we could hope for was an appointment next week. And it's great news that he can marry us on the fourteenth.'

'I know, but that's because it falls on a Thursday and most people want to get married on a Saturday. I hope it doesn't stop anyone from attending.'

'Will you stop finding things to worry about. I'm sure that everyone who's important to you will find a way to be there.'

'Just as long as you are,' joked Kate.

'I'll think about it,' laughed Max as he cowered to avoid the half-expected blow from his intended.

At that moment a smartly dressed middle-aged man approached them. 'Mr. Sherwood and Miss Hart?'

Max nodded, stood up and offered his hand.

After shaking hands, the man sat down in a vacant chair beside them. 'I'm Mr Hunter, the duty manager. How may I help you?'

Max explained the situation but as soon as he mentioned the date Mr Hunter sucked in a large amount of air through pursed lips and said, 'Unfortunately we already have a Valentines' Dinner Party booked for that evening.'

He noticed the immense disappointment on Kates' face and added, 'but leave it with me. I'll confirm the numbers of this booking and see if it would be possible to move them to our Restaurant thus freeing up our Ballroom. I'll call you early next week with an answer.'

Kates' smile lit up her face so brilliantly that he felt the need to add a note of caution directly towards her.

'I can't promise anything of course, and it may yet still prove to be impossible.'

'I understand,' replied Kate. 'But thank-you for trying.'

As they left Kate turned to Max and said, 'Fingers crossed that he'll be able to sort it out for us because I don't know where else we could go if he doesn't. I think he was touched that we liked his hotel so much.'

'Oh Kate, don't set your heart on this place too much darling,' he said gently, inwardly hurting because he couldn't guarantee this for her. ' I'm sure we'll find somewhere else just as nice if we have to.'

Knowing that Kate wouldn't view anywhere else with an open mind while the Excelsior was still a possibility and that, if they were to call it a day now, she would keep mulling the situation over in her mind *ad infinitum,* until she became thoroughly depressed, Max came up with a distraction.

'Anyway, we can't do anymore planning today so let's go shopping for the wedding rings.'

As they walked towards the car, Kate's spirits lifted immediately as she explained her ideas about the type of wedding bands that she had in mind. 'I was thinking of matching wide D shaped rings with our names engraved on the inside....'

Max merely smiled indulgently as he opened her car door.

*　　*　　*　　*　　*

Gina looked at Leanne and then at Ross and shook her head. 'No, I need you to tell me now. What's wrong? What's happened?' her voice was almost shrill.

Leanne started to cry and Ross moved towards them both.

'Just say it please,' begged Gina, sitting herself down at the bottom of the stairs. 'Its Matt, isn't it? He's had an accident.'

Ross nodded miserably. 'This is the hardest thing I've *ever* had to do, Gina,' he said quietly and sat down beside her, as Leanne continued to cry.

'Please, please tell me that he isn't dead. Please, please, God,' Gina's imploring eyes filled with horror when Ross did not hurry to reassure her that this was not the case.

'I'm so sorry Gina but he was killed on his motorbike as he ...'

The scream that came from Gina's lips was as if she were dying herself. Leanne tried to comfort her but she was inconsolable and collapsed in a heap on the floor, sobbing and screaming until there were no more tears. Eventually, she managed to compose herself enough to hug Leanne and to find out exactly what had happened.

'We don't know the precise details yet but he was riding with his friends on a winding mountain road and swerved to avoid a car coming in the opposite direction. He skidded off and was killed instantly.'

Gina could not take in the word "killed" and grasping at straws suddenly offered a slither of hope.

'But how do we know for sure that it was him? You hear about this sort of thing all the time. People make mistakes about identity,' and then she started to break down again and whispered, 'How do you know for sure? I loved him so much. It can't be him.'

'Oh Gina. We do know for sure. One of his friends called us early this morning to tell us what had happened.'

Gina fell back to the floor. Everything was surreal. It was as if a big switch had been turned off and taken all the life out of her body. She didn't know what to do with herself and just wanted it to be last week again so that she could alter the events and bring him back to her.

'I should have stopped him. It's my fault. I knew something bad was going to happen. I just felt it and I should have listened to what it was trying to tell me. I should have stopped him, Leanne. I should have said he couldn't go on holiday and even if he'd hated me afterwards, at least he would still be alive. Oh my God. How am I going to live without him?'

Leanne and Gina hugged and cried for several minutes while Ross made them both a cup of tea.

'Ross is going to make all the arrangements Gina. My lovely brother is going to be home soon, and then we can say our final goodbyes.'

Ross returned with the tea. 'Is there anybody else you want us to call?'

Gina suddenly put on her bravest of faces and shook her head.

'No. I want to be alone thanks. I hope you don't mind but I'll let my family know when I'm ready. Oh, I need someone to pick up Kieran from school, so if you could call my mum and ask her to do it, that would be useful.'

'Of course,' assured Ross. 'If you're positive about this, then I'll call her as soon as we get home.'

Gina got a pen and piece of paper from the kitchen and wrote down her parent's number.

'Please, don't tell her. Just say I can't pick him up and would she take Kieran back to hers. I'll explain to her later.' She smiled weakly, thanked them both for telling her to her face and walked back into the lounge.

CHAPTER 20

Kate and Max lay entwined on his sofa watching an international football match on the television. Kate, not being a great soccer fan, was gazing around Max's sitting room, admiring his taste. The Swedish black ash furniture contrasted beautifully with the cream soft furnishings and could have looked severe save for a large luscious pot plant, a striking abstract painting in earthy tones on the feature wall and the palest peach hue colouring the walls and creating a subtle warm glow. The bookcase was full of a mixture of sporting and financial tomes along with an impressive array of sporting trophies. Although obviously a masculine bachelor pad, Kate could see that their tastes were not that far apart and that the home they were about to set up together would be tastefully and exquisitely furnished. She was mulling over possible styles and colour schemes when the phone ringing interrupted her thoughts. Max, irritated that someone would be stupid enough to phone during the televised match, picked up the receiver and abruptly answered 'Hello'.

After a short silence in which his whole demeanour softened, he handed the receiver to Kate saying

   'It's Gina, for you darling. She's in a terrible state, I think something is seriously wrong.'

Kate virtually snatched the phone from Max and asked urgently, 'Hi Gina, what's wrong darling?'

Kate sat stunned as Gina blurted out that Matt was dead and explained through her sobbing and tears how it had all happened.

Kate's immediate response was to say 'I'm coming round now, I'll be there in a few minutes.'

'No Kate. Thank-you, but no,' Gina refused adamantly. 'I know you're only trying to help but I need to be alone. Kieran's with Mum and I need this time by myself. You do understand, don't you?'

'Of course I do Gina,' assured Kate but added 'It's just that I'll be worrying about you, that's all. If you change your mind or if you just want to talk, you know where I am. Just phone me, any time of the day or night, I mean it, okay? So phone me, promise?'

'I promise,' whispered a distraught Gina.

The pain in her friend's voice churned the very pit of Kates' stomach and she added 'Look after yourself, Gina. I love you and I'm here if you need me.'

'Thank-you Kate,' Gina's voice broke again into a sob. 'I've got to go, bye.' And she hung up before Kate had a chance to reply.

Kate stared at Max with a mixture of bewilderment and disbelief in her eyes and Max looked back at her, patiently waiting for her to explain the phone call.

'This is so surreal,' Kate began as she relayed Gina's terrible news. 'I can't believe it's happened, they were so perfect together. We used to compare notes about how happy we both were and compete with each other over who had the more perfect man.'

Max looked down, uncomfortable with this inappropriately timed compliment.

'And now it's all been snatched away from her. I can't begin to imagine the pain she's in. It's so unfair...' Kate trailed into a silence and was lost in thought for a few moments before she suddenly announced 'Max, we'll have to postpone the wedding. It wouldn't be fair on Gina. It would be like rubbing salt into the wound to carry on with the arrangements while her heart is breaking. I can't do that to her.'

'Slow down a bit,' interrupted Max. 'I understand what you are saying and to a certain extent I agree with you, but I think you should wait until you see Gina. It's early days and Gina is still trying to get over the shock. You never know she might want to throw herself into helping you as her way of dealing with this; you know, something else for her to think about. To be honest I doubt it, although Gina is a very determined woman, so nothing she did would surprise me. Anyway, what I'm trying to say, is before you make a hasty decision, wait until you have seen Gina and take your lead from her. Whatever you decide will be fine by me.'

'Thank-you Max,' half-smiled Kate and the look in her eyes spoke volumes of the love she felt for this understanding and considerate man.

*   *   *   *   *

Gina thought that going to work would help her to get through the day but in fact, matters had been made much worse. Every file she looked at spoke of a time when Matt was still alive. Every step of her journey was pure torture as she was reminded of gloriously happy times with Matt. She regretted leaving the house as soon as she had stepped on the bus but decided to try to throw herself into her work and then see how she felt at lunch break. Richard arrived at the office mid morning and was horrified to see her sitting at her desk, promptly insisting on taking her for breakfast and then driving her home. He had offered plenty of words of comfort but nothing could even touch the edges of her grief let alone console her and as she almost choked on the eggs and bacon he had ordered, she burst into tears. Richard hugged her tightly as she cried and cried.

On returning home she thanked Richard and assured him that she preferred to be alone. He left only after she'd promised that she would not even think about working again until after the funeral. She flopped onto a chair and just stared out at the room in front of her, shaking her head in disbelief and at the injustice of it all. After several minutes her mother rang to suggest that Kieran stay with his grandparents again that evening, and Gina agreed knowing that she would not be able to put on a brave face, not even for Kieran. *After the funeral I'll be able to cope better,* she thought to herself.

She spent the rest of the morning reading all of Matt's cards and letters that he had sent her, and wearing the one shirt that he had left behind on one of his overnight stays. It still smelt of his after-shave and every few minutes she brought the collar up to her nose as she read his romantic words over and over again. She alternated between smiles and tears as she touched the treasured pieces of paper with her fingertips and looked at the few photographs that she had collated in their short time together.

Not knowing what to do with the rest of her day, she ran a bath and poured lots of lavender bubble gel into the running water. Tears were welling up inside her and she needed the comfort of the hot soapy water in which to allow them to run into. She had just turned the taps off when the phone rang again.

'Hi Gina, it's me, Kate. Do you want some company this evening?'

Gina hesitated. 'I'm sorry Kate, I know it must be hard for everyone to know what to do but I really do want to be on my own. I just don't feel like making conversation and I don't want you sitting here watching me cry all evening. But I do appreciate your offer. Claire asked me the same thing yesterday and I've said no to her as well, so please don't think it's just you.'

'I don't mind if you cry. I'll just be there to hand you the tissues if you like. We're all worried about you and I'm not sure you're eating anything. What if I just come round for an hour or so and bring a take-away with me?'

'That's a lovely thought but I really couldn't eat anything. Honestly Kate, thanks again but I really need time to take this all in. I'll give you a call in a couple of days. I'll need you more next week when it's the day of the....' she trailed off not able to say the words and slowly replaced the phone onto the receiver. She felt awful but at this moment there was no room for consideration of anyone else. She was void of any emotion except that of anger, despair and helplessness. Only her mother could provide her with any sort of comfort and that is where she would head for, if anywhere.

As she lay in the bath she admitted to herself that she couldn't bear to see her two best friends at the moment, partly because she preferred to be alone but also because they were both so happy with the men they loved. The jealousy was profound, in a way that she didn't think could be possible, and although it wasn't their fault that this had happened, it all seemed so unfair that it was she who had lost her soul mate. As she played with the bubbles, she suddenly remembered the time that Matt had invited himself to join her in the bath and she smiled for a moment, lost in the magic of his touch and the sound of his silken voice. It was a brief reprieve from her heavy heart and when her mind fought its way back to the present, the grief just overwhelmed her. She cried out and screamed into the steamy air, splashing the water hard with her fist before succumbing to the heavy sobs that were now part of her day, morning, noon and night.

*   *   *   *   *

Kate phoned Gina every morning to check on her friend and when, a couple of days later, Gina announced that Kieran was coming home tomorrow she knew that it would be safe to visit, that she would not be imposing on her friend's private grief. She immediately phoned Max to explain that as she was going to visit Gina straight after work she would probably be late home and thus unable to see him as previously arranged. Max was, as usual, totally accommodating about this change of plan but insisted that Kate get a hot meal at lunchtime as she might not get a chance to that evening. Kate, touched by his concern, assured him she would be fine, as it was one of her intentions to ensure that her best friend got a good meal inside her as she was pretty convinced that she wouldn't have been eating properly. After making arrangements to see each other the following evening they said their goodbyes. Kate visited the local supermarket during her lunch-hour to buy the ingredients for the meal she intended to cook for Gina that evening. After school she hurriedly completed her preparation for the following day's lessons before driving straight round to Gina's house.

The sight that greeted Kate on the doorstep totally shocked her. She had expected to see Gina looking dishevelled and tired, even a little gaunt. She did not, however, expect her to look so ill, so grey in colour and so thin. She wondered how anyone could lose so much weight so quickly.

'Oh Gina,' she said as she hugged her friend tightly and stroked her back. 'I don't know what to say.'

'There isn't anything you can say Kate, this hug is enough,' replied Gina with genuine emotion at being reunited with her friend.

As the two women walked into the house and the kitchen, Kate said, 'I've taken the liberty of bringing along our supper,' and held up the supermarket carrier bags in evidence. 'I thought I could cook and give you an evening off.'

Gina smiled as best she could but it was somewhat half-hearted. She turned on the kettle and proceeded to make two mugs of coffee and Kate was again shocked to see how listless Gina appeared. It was almost as if she was a robot or on autopilot, there was no animation about her, no personality shining through.

Kate thanked Gina for the coffee and the two friends sat at the kitchen table sipping their drinks in silence, a silence that Kate found awkward. She broke it by saying 'You stay there while I start on our supper,' and immediately began to prepare the meal in the kitchen she knew almost as well as her own. She was relieved to be doing something, as she felt strangely uncomfortable. It was not that she didn't know what to say, a problem she had experienced in the past when faced with a grieving person, as their friendship was deep enough for this not to be an issue. It was as though Gina had put up a barrier that she could not penetrate. She was distant and flat despite the warmth of her welcome when Kate had first arrived. Kate chastised herself for being so selfish. *Of course Gina is distant*, she thought to herself. *She has just lost the love of her life and her mind is in turmoil.*

Kate tried to make conversation as she cooked but Gina's replies were brief and to the point.

'How's Kieran?'

'He's fine.'

'Do you need any help with him?'

'No thanks, he's been spending quite a bit of time with his Dad.'

'Do you need any help with grocery shopping or laundry or anything?'

It's okay, mum's helping out.'

'Oh Gina, is there *anything* I can do?'

'No, not unless you can bring back the dead,' replied Gina sardonically and almost bitterly, as tears pricked her eyes and she stared into the middle distance.

Kate completed the meal in silence, served it up and placed a plate in front of Gina adding,

'There you are darling, tuck in.'

She sat opposite her friend and started to eat. She noticed that Gina was pushing the food around her plate and actually eating very little.

'Come on Gina dear, you've got to eat or you'll make yourself ill,' cajoled Kate.

'You sound just like my mother Kate, but I can't, it just chokes me,' she replied giving yet another half-hearted smile.

Seeing her friend so distraught, Kate knew she couldn't go ahead with her wedding, expecting Gina to be a part of it, so she made the decision there and then and announced 'Max and I have decided to postpone our wedding, just for a little while,' Kate smiled as she clasped Gina's hand.

'You don't have to for my sake,' Gina answered and although the protest was genuine, Kate could sense her relief. Kate felt the need to elaborate on her decision so Gina did not take on the burden of having her friend change her plans for her sake.

'Anyway, Howard is up to his old tricks again and I really can't concentrate on wedding plans while I'm trying to deal with him,' she added, little realising that this innocent lie would prove to be so prophetic.

Kate spent the rest of the evening with Gina, comforting her when she cried, sitting quietly when she was lost in her thoughts and chatting when Gina instigated a conversation. One of these was to impart the details of Matt's forthcoming funeral. She explained that Leanne had insisted on Gina playing a significant part in the planning as Matt would have wanted it that way and she was grateful to have been included. She added, almost pleadingly to Kate, 'You will be there, wont you? Matt deserves the best send off we can give him,' and then sunk into another of her thoughtful silences. When an almost visible wave of exhaustion washed over Gina, Kate suggested she went to bed, as she looked awfully tired. She declined Kate's offer to stay the night or to make her a hot milky drink saying that once Kate left she would be heading straight to bed. Kate took the hint and left immediately saying that she would phone her as usual the following day.

Once back at home, and although it was quite late, Kate phoned Max to tell him about the evening and her decision to postpone the wedding. Max said he'd book the time off for the funeral and that they could talk things through in more detail tomorrow evening, as he really must get some sleep now and so should she. After saying their goodnights Kate immediately went up to bed but her mind was so full of thoughts of her poor heart-broken friend that sleep was a long time coming.

CHAPTER 21

How Gina got through the days leading up to the funeral, she would never know. The whole time was spent in robot mode, eating and drinking from necessity and spending most of her time with her parents and Kieran. The day she had dreaded most had arrived and any energy she had was used to prepare herself physically and emotionally for the outside world. As she took one last look in the mirror, she saw an empty shell of a woman stare back at her. She had lost over half a stone in weight and it showed. Her gaunt face held empty eyes and quivering lips. Her olive skin, once glowing with the ecstasy of being in love, was yellow and pale. Determined to hold it together, at least until the funeral was underway, she turned her thoughts to the poem she had put together for Matt. She took out the piece of paper from her handbag and read the words to herself, quietly acknowledging that she would have to take up Richard's offer to read them out for her at the service. There was no way she would get through to the end without breaking down. She really wanted to do this for Matt and had told Richard that she would call on him at the last moment if she really felt that she could not cope. This was still her plan but reading the words again just brought home the awful reality that she would never see him again and it was just unbearable. She had loved him so much.

The knock on the door made Gina jump. She picked up her belongings and made her way to the front door where the now familiar shape of Ross was visible. She was relieved to leave the emptiness of her house.

'Hi Ross, thanks for coming to pick me up,' she managed a smile and kissed him on the cheek.

He opened the door of his car. 'It's no bother at all Gina. How are you bearing up?'

'Not good Ross but then I don't suppose anybody is. I just want the day to be over and done with.'

Ross looked tired and weary. 'Leanne is not good this morning. She's trying to be brave for her parent's sake but is finding it difficult. I'm sure you'll help each other.'

They arrived at the house just half an hour before the hearse was due and it seemed an eternity before Matt arrived. The sun glinted on the shiny white coffin, which was surrounded by the most beautiful flowers and wreaths.

'Oh God. He's here,' Leanne murmured as she turned to look at Gina helplessly.

'It's okay. It's okay,' Gina reassured gently. 'Let's go and be with him.'

Ross, Leanne, Matt's parents and Gina walked slowly to the car, hesitating briefly to look at the flowers before taking their place by his side for the long, deliberate ride to the church. The conversation on the way to the church was false and trivial as if they were all pretending that they were going on a normal journey to nowhere in particular. There was even talk about the outfits they were wearing and how Leanne hoped there was enough food for everyone back at the house. It was so surreal. These moments of denial were regularly interrupted by the expressions on the faces of people standing in the street, some making the sign of the cross as they watched Matt leave the neighbourhood where he had spent most of his life, for one last time.

There seemed to be hundreds of people waiting at the church for Matt's arrival. This was no surprise as he had always been popular and had many close friends. It was a great source of comfort to his family to see the people whose lives he had enriched, coming together for a final goodbye. As the coffin was carried in to Matt's favourite song, "You'll Never Walk Alone," Gina could no longer hold back the tears. She joined Claire and Richard who were waiting to comfort her at the front of the church but she couldn't look at them. The pain running through her body was like an invisible force pushing down on her from every direction, suffocating her and making her want to scream out loud. As long as she didn't look at the pity in everybody's eyes, she would be strong.

The service was beautiful and the priest said all the right things at the right time. Not being a religious person, Gina took very little comfort from his words but she did feel that this was not the end and that Matt was with her every step of the way. Suddenly she found the strength to read her poem and nodded to Richard that she was okay. He put his hand on hers and gave a reassuring squeeze before she stood up to publicly share her love for Matt with everyone that had known him.

My World

'When our eyes first met, my world stood still – I saw no other.

When we first met, the music faded – I heard no other

When you became part of my life, I knew we were made for each other

When we fell in love, my head was spinning – I felt no other

When there were problems, these were shared – I needed no other

When you were taken from us – My world just stopped.

I thank-you for the precious time we spent – loving each other

God Bless you Matt. You are forever in my heart'

The steps between saying her public goodbye to finding herself looking down at his final resting-place were taken in a complete daze.

Kate and Max stood at the back of the graveyard behind the large crowd of mourners. Max held a protective arm around Kate's shoulder. Kate looked through the crowd at Gina, her reddened eyes and trembling frame a testament to her all consuming grief. Although being comforted by both Leanne and Ross she looked so isolated and alone. Kate felt so helpless and removed from her friend and wished she could be there for her. But at that precise moment, the agonising truth dawned on Kate. It was not just the crowd that was keeping the friends apart, it was that for the first time in their friendship their lives were not running a parallel course. They were in two such very different places that they were now no longer at one with one another. Although Kate was offering sympathy and comfort to Gina, the happiness and contentment in her heart blocked their once natural empathy. Equally the all-enveloping grief swallowing Gina was a bar on her sharing Kate's bright future, one that until recently they had both had. Tears began to run silently down Kate's cheeks. She was mourning not just for Matt and the pain of her dearest friend, but for the temporary loss of their friendship. She would take a step back, keep her distance to make it easier for Gina, but be there for her should she need her and be ready with open arms when her friend was ready to come back to her. As though reading her thoughts, Max, at that moment, tightened his arm around Kate.

Although the school day was over by the time the funeral had ended, Kate returned to work to prepare for the following day. She was in the resources room searching for some work sheets when Howard came in.

'Oh, hello Kate, I didn't expect you back today. Can't keep away from us, eh?' he leered.

'Hello Howard,' she groaned. 'I've got 4C first thing tomorrow and I hadn't got anything ready,' she added by way of explanation.

'How did the funeral go?' he asked, trying to strike up a conversation that Kate really didn't want.

'As well as a funeral can go,' she replied dismissively.

'Well I admire your dedication to duty,' he smirked as he moved closer.

'Please Howard, don't. I can't handle a confrontation today of all days.'

'Oh, touchy. Methinks the lady doth protest too much,' he added as his smirk turned into a sneer.

'Howard, don't start all this again. I thought we had sorted all this out.' The tension was rising in her voice as she spoke.

'All what?' He queried in mock innocence. 'I didn't think we had anything to sort out.' And at that moment he lunged towards her pressing himself against her and adding 'Oh, come on, just once, you never know, you might even enjoy it.'

As he tried to kiss her, Kate managed to wriggle free and ran out of the room and down the corridor, his laughter fading as the distance grew between them. On spotting the team of school cleaners, Kate immediately felt much safer and was able to compose herself before they noticed her. She popped into her classroom to collect her coat and bags, said goodnight to the group of women and hurried to her car. She drove straight round to Max's and once he had let her in, she burst into tears as she relayed the entire sordid incident.

*   *   *   *   *

A week later Kate was sitting in the passenger seat of Max's car as he drove to the County Hotel.

'I don't want to do this,' she stated out of the blue.

'Oh come on, it wont be that bad,' replied Max. 'You'll be fine and I'll be with you all the time.' There was a short silence as he manoeuvred through some road works. 'Anyway,' he added 'It would look really odd if you didn't show up to the staff's annual Christmas dinner.'

'I know I'm being silly, but I've managed to avoid Howard totally since last week and the last thing I want to do is to socialise with him.'

'Actually, this is probably the best way to see him again. I mean he's hardly going to try anything, what with his wife and me there. Is he?'

'I'm not so sure,' answered Kate.

I am,' replied a determined Max.

As Kate and Max entered the ballroom, they were immediately spotted by Stephanie who waved excitedly and beckoned them over, indicating at the two vacant places she had reserved for them. She introduced them to James, her date for the evening, but then in a whispered aside to Kate, added, 'Don't bother with him too much, he won't be around for long.'

Stephanie had gathered the most fun-loving members of staff together, at their table. There were her two male colleagues from the PE department, Jason and Rob, along with their girlfriends. They were sat next to Eloise Dupont, the young French teacher and her boyfriend on one side, and Martin Davidson, the new art teacher and his very bohemian and pregnant wife, on the other.

After exchanging warm greetings Kate sat down and was immediately relieved to see that Howard was at the other end of the room with the rest of the senior staff. Kate relaxed and as the meal progressed she began to really enjoy herself as she and her colleagues exchanged comical anecdotes. Schools are generally awash with humorous incidents and, as theirs was no exception, the funny stories kept on coming. Even the partners, who on such occasions can often feel left out, were enjoying the banter. Once the meal was over and the music was playing, their group continued to enjoy each other's company on the dance floor.

Towards the end of the evening, Kate noticed that Max's trip to the 'Gents' was taking rather longer than it should. Concerned that he was all right she went in search of him and stopped abruptly outside the men's toilets when she heard raised voices and a scuffle. After a few minutes a petrified looking Howard came scurrying out holding a handkerchief to his bloodied nose. Moment's later Max emerged straightening his tie in a pastiche of a scene from a James Bond movie.

'What on earth's been going on? Kate asked trying to appear shocked but finding it hard to conceal her amusement.

'Howard won't be troubling you again,' replied an almost comically assertive Max.

'But what happened in there?' pressed Kate.

'Let's just say this was a Christmas Bash in more ways than one.'

As her Knight in shining armour guided her back into the dance hall, Kate's grin was a mixture of admiration and amusement.

*   *   *   *   *

Although Kate had spoken to Gina every day since the funeral, it was over the telephone and she had not actually seen her. It was because of this that she now felt a strange trepidation as she walked up the path to her front door. Kate was on her Christmas vacation and as she knew Gina would be at home with Kieran she had arranged to visit her this Tuesday afternoon to deliver her Christmas gifts. Kate braced herself as she rang the doorbell but as the door opened Gina immediately threw her arms around her friend and proclaimed 'Kate, It's so good to see you.'

Kate instantly relaxed and was relieved to see Gina looking so much better. She was still a little thin and there was still a sadness in her eyes but she had made her usual effort with her appearance and her smile was warm and genuine. As Gina made coffee, an over-excited Kieran climbed all over his Auntie Kate as they played their usual little game of Kate denying that she had bought him anything and him refusing to believe her. He would then search her pockets until she finally gave in and produced a bag of sweets for him from her bag. Gina gave her full attention to her young son when he asked if he could eat them now and with an affirmative answer he went back into the sitting room to watch cartoons on the television, while Gina joined Kate at the kitchen table.

Kate looked at Gina and smiled warmly. 'You look so much better Gina. How are you keeping?'

'Not too badly,' Gina sighed. 'I have my moments but I've got to keep positive for Kieran's sake.'

'Well, he's certainly full of beans at the moment but it's not all too much for you, is it?' asked a concerned Kate.

'On the contrary Kate, Kieran's so excited about Christmas he's just the distraction I need,' Gina paused before adding reflectively, 'I'm not looking forward to it, though.'

'I can imagine,' replied Kate and as a worried expression appeared on her face, she asked 'You're not going to be alone, though, are you?'

'Oh no,' assured Gina. 'Mum is planning her usual family gathering and we're staying over, *and* we've also been invited to spend some time with Leanne and Ross.'

'Are you going?'

'Probably, but I'll see how I feel nearer the time. If not, I'll just stay with Mum a bit longer,' replied Gina and then added, 'Anyway, I don't want to think about all that now so let's change the subject.'

'Of course,' answered an almost chastised Kate and then, in an attempt to lighten the mood, she over exaggerated her turn towards Gina and added, 'I think I can guess what you *do* want to talk about?'

Gina leaned towards Kate conspiratorially and replied. 'Well yes, what I really want to know is…what has been going on with Howard? Over the phone you mentioned an altercation and that it's now all been sorted out, but I want all the gory details please.'

'Well,' smiled Kate as she leaned back into her chair and let her story telling prowess go into free fall. 'It started when I was in the resources room after school one day…'

She proceeded to explain the incident in detail, but avoided any reference to the funeral so as not to adversely affect Gina's mood. Gina looked suitably shocked but her expression turned to one of amusement when Kate went on to relay the night of the Christmas dinner. By the time Kate was explaining the scene outside the Gent's toilets they were both laughing aloud particularly when Kate ended her story by saying 'And since that night Max has been taking his Martinis shaken, not stirred.'

The girls spent the remainder of the afternoon in easy harmony and when they parted they promised to get together again soon after the Christmas break. Kate drove home to prepare a meal for Max in buoyant mood. Not only had she had an enjoyable afternoon with her best friend but for the first time in a long while she could think about Gina without worrying. True, her friend was still grieving, but she was beginning to cope with her situation and she knew that given time her friend was strong enough to be able to move on.

CHAPTER 22

Christmas day started quietly. Kieran had decided to be with his dad the night before and to wake up to lots of presents from Joe and his close relatives. It was tradition in Gina's family to wait until they were all together before being allowed to open all of the presents. This meant that Kieran would have woken to merely a few gifts from Gina herself and so she had given him the option of where he wanted to spend the night. Nothing mattered more than for her excited child to have a normal Christmas full of fun and anticipation. She had agreed with Joe that Kieran would then spend the rest of Christmas Day and Boxing Day with her, and Joe had promised to drop him off at 11am. For Gina it had seemed an eternity since she had last seen Kieran. With no cooking to do and no presents to open, except for one from Kieran which she had left until he could give it to her personally, she felt lost and alone. Looking out of the window, coffee in one hand and her earlier-than-usual morning cigarette in the other, she saw several children emerging from their homes, proudly clutching their new toys. Skates, bikes, prams and remote controlled cars suddenly appeared, bringing the street alive with noisy chatter and shrieking excitement. She smiled for a moment as she thought of the football assortment she had paid a fortune for, including a ball that was kindly signed by the local team, a shirt and various books. He was going to be over the moon. At least she had been able to afford his second choice, leaving Joe to buy the selection of games and toys that Kieran had hinted about for no less than half the year. Her thoughts then turned to Leanne and she decided to call her to let her know that she would be popping round to see her the next day and to wish her a Merry Christmas. Except it was never, ever going to be that and so, having lifted the receiver, she hesitated and decided to think some more about the words she was going to use.

'Have a satisfactory, reasonable, best that you can in the circumstances Christmas?' Gina said almost sarcastically to herself. No, there were no right words and none that she herself would want to hear from anyone so she replaced the receiver, deciding to leave it and just turn up tomorrow when half of this unwelcome holiday was over.

After a long hot shower she dressed herself in an outfit, bought especially for the occasion, and lightly applied makeup to give her face a much-needed lift. At this moment there wasn't anyone to look beautiful for but she wanted to appear normal and happy to her family. She spent the rest of her time laying out the presents onto the floor in readiness for Kieran's arrival and decorated the tree with some new baubles that she had seen in the market.

Joe arrived punctually and asked if he could come into the house for a while. Gina had found him sensitive and thoughtful since Matt had died. He seemed genuinely sorry for her and had been especially helpful by looking after Kieran overnight when he thought that Gina looked worn out. She welcomed him in.

After all the presents were opened, Joe asked if he could have a private word and the opportunity to do that soon came when Kieran went into his bedroom and laid out all his new additions next to his prized collection of sporting paraphernalia.

'So, what is it you want to tell me?' she asked as she offered Joe a chocolate novelty from the tree.

'No, thanks. I'm trying to save myself for the turkey,' he smiled back.

'Rightly so. So where are you getting fed today? Round your mum's, I presume?'

'Well, that's what I wanted to talk to you about,' he replied nervously.

'Ah, you've written a will in case she kills you off with her cooking,' Gina quipped, remembering the last time they'd had Christmas dinner at his mothers and had been struck down with food poisoning. 'It's okay, you can leave everything to Kieran, I don't mind.'

Joe remained serious and Gina, sensing that the joking may not be appropriate, continued, 'Sorry Joe, you're trying to tell me something important aren't you?'

'Oh don't worry,' he reassured. 'It's nothing to worry about. I just wanted to let you know that I'm seeing someone else and that her name is Cathy and I would like Joe to meet her soon.'

The words couldn't tumble out of his mouth quick enough.

Gina stared incredulously at her ex husband. She wasn't sure what emotion she was feeling but it resembled close to a form of betrayal. Although she was sensible enough to know that he had been a free agent for months, she had never expected to be replaced so soon. There was no way that she ever wanted to go back to Joe but the thought of Kieran having a substitute mother at the weekends was not what she needed or expected to face right now. Nothing came from her lips as she continued to look surprised and caught off guard.

'Are you okay?' he asked. 'You weren't expecting me to wait for you forever, were you?'

Gina shook her head and he continued, 'Well then what's wrong? I gave up hope when Matt came along and the divorce papers came through. So please don't make me feel guilty about this.'

'Of course you mustn't feel bad. I'm glad that you've found happiness again and I don't begrudge it one little bit. It's just that I need to meet this

Cathy if I'm to entrust her with Kieran's welfare – that's all.' Gina stood up letting him know that it was time to go now and thank you very much.

'Fair enough but let's not get ahead of ourselves here. We're only dating at the moment so there's no need for you to worry about that just yet.'

And with that he kissed her on the cheek, shouted his goodbyes to Kieran and left.

The remaining days were a bit of a blur to Gina. Much to her mother's concern, she had decided to consume several glasses of wine, in an effort to minimise her pain, and this was not like Gina at all. The family did not drink alcohol over Christmas, preferring to use any spare capacity in their bodies for even more food but Gina needed to dull her senses in order to survive the meaningless celebrations and join, at least in part, with some of the days activities. Boxing day was better but she was left in no doubt that the healing was going to take months not weeks before she was ready to be totally at peace with her life again. Leanne and Ross made the best of it and provided Gina with some comfort as they talked about Matt and all the funny things he did as a child. It wasn't just a question of remembering only the good about him. He truly had been a fantastic brother, son, friend and lover.

'Now that he's in heaven, I'll have to look after you again, won't I mummy?' Kieran had said during one of the many conversations about Matt.

Leanne just smiled and replied with a nod, prompting Ross to quickly change the subject. Gina pushed her grief to the back of mind and subconsciously pretended that Matt was in another room, just as he had been on that very first evening when she had helped Leanne to clear up the kitchen as the men relaxed in the lounge.

Ross was fantastic, cooking the meal and playing with Kieran while the two girls chatted. The evening was rounded off with a game of cards, which Kieran won, and when Leanne insisted that they both stay the night in the spare room, Gina was too exhausted to refuse. That night she slept soundly for the first time in months, having spent several hours talking about the man she loved and downing more alcohol in the form of brandy and babychams. She noted the next morning that it was also the first time that she had not cried, at least once, the whole day. Perhaps there was a tiny glimmer that, at last, she could now look forward to the New Year and her best friend's wedding, amongst other things, without feeling resentful.

*   *   *   *   *

It was the day after Boxing Day and Kate and Max were relaxing in her sitting room reading the first daily newspapers for two days. They had spent Christmas Day with her family and yesterday with his and were enjoying a quieter day alone together. Max stirred and went into the kitchen, emerging a few minutes later with two coffees. Handing one to Kate he announced 'I've been thinking.'

'That's dangerous,' grinned Kate.

Max mocked a hurt expression as he sat down beside her on the sofa adding 'Seriously, I think we ought to start re-booking our wedding. We've agreed an Easter wedding would be nice and now Gina is stronger I'm sure it would be okay to go ahead. I mean it's a decent time period since Matt's funeral...'

'I think you're right,' interrupted Kate sensing his awkwardness at mentioning a possibly sensitive subject.

'I'm so glad you do,' he sighed with relief and then went on, 'Because if we leave it much longer we could encounter the same problems as we did the last time.'

'I couldn't agree more, so we'd better get organised.' The schoolteacher in Kate came to the fore as she rose to retrieve a pen and pad from her bureau and then sat down again before writing on the top of a clean sheet of paper: *Wedding- Things To Do.*

Together she and Max compiled a list of all the things they needed to organise and when they were satisfied that they hadn't forgotten anything they focused on the one point on which everything else depended; booking the church. After a short debate as to whether it would be appropriate to phone the vicar that day, Max took the bull by the horns and phoned. The vicar, who was as charming as he was the first time they had approached him, agreed to a meeting in two days time. With that fixed, Kate and Max continued to add meat to the bones of their list, checking the phone directory for possible stationers, florists and the like. They spent their entire day planning and organising as much as they could and by the time they went to bed no stone had been left unturned.

Two days later they were sitting in the vicar's office discussing the details of their big day. Easter Saturday at 2pm was confirmed and hymns and readings were chosen. They also arranged the dates and times for their spiritual guidance meetings, something most faiths embark upon, in order to impress upon couples the sanctity of holy matrimony, and something which Max and Kate were happy to comply with.

Having booked the serious aspect of the day, Max and Kate then visited the Excelsior Hotel to book the reception. They again saw Mr. Hunter who this time was able to confirm immediately that the ballroom was available for hire on Easter Saturday. Once they had confirmed the booking Mr. Hunter called upon the chef to discuss details about the catering for the wedding breakfast.

As they walked back to the car the ever-efficient Kate referred once more to her list.

'Where to next?' asked Max.

'Only four things left to do, the stationery, the cake, the flowers and the cars, so back towards town. We pass the car hire place on our way, so it makes sense to go their first,' Kate answered.

'Right you are, boss,' mocked Max affectionately as he tugged at his imaginary cap.

Once the limousines had been booked, it was onto the printers to choose and order the stationery, then to the specialist bakers and finally the florists to do likewise with the wedding cake and the flowers. As they got back into the car for the last time, relieved that it was all done, Max turned to Kate.

'Would you like to go and tell Gina?'

'What, now?' asked Kate, pausing only momentarily. 'Yes, please.'

As Gina opened her door to the two of them, they greeted each other warmly before Gina added, 'This is an unexpected surprise,' as she lead them into her sitting room.

'We've got something to tell you,' replied a tentative Kate.

Sensing her anxiety Gina cajoled, 'Well, spit it out then.'

'We've set the wedding date, Easter Saturday. We've just spent the entire day booking up everything.'

'Oh, that's fantastic, it's great to hear some good news for a change. I was going to offer you a coffee but I think this deserves something stronger. How about a glass of wine?' asked Gina.

'That would be great, thanks, but I've got one favour to ask first,' added Kate.

'What's that?' Gina stopped in her tracks.

'Would you be my matron of honour?'

The tears welled up in Gina's eyes and she gave her friend the biggest hug. 'I'd be honoured. Nobody deserves this more than you,' she whispered into Kate's ear. Kate was overcome by the magnanimity of her dearest friend who had been through so much and hugged her back with equal affection.

PART THREE

NEW BEGINNINGS

CHAPTER 23

Kate was in her bedroom and had just finished the last touches to her make-up, when the phone rang.

'Hi darling, it's me,' greeted Kate's mum.

'Hiya, mum,' replied Kate cheerfully.

'I'm sorry to have to do this at such short notice, dear, but both your dad and I have caught this terrible flu bug that's going around and I'm really not up to going shopping today.'

'Oh, no mum,' Kate sounded disappointed.

'But you and Gina can go ahead without me.'

Kate protested. 'Yes I know but it's part of a mother's role to help her daughter choose her wedding dress.'

'Kate, darling,' replied her mother in her most matriarchal tone. 'It's been years since you've ever taken any notice of anything I have had to say and I'm sure that you're quite definite about what you plan to wear anyway.'

'Oh, well, if you put it like that then I'm sure Gina and I will cope quite admirably,' replied Kate smartly.

'Oh, don't be like that darling. You know that's not what I meant. And I know that you'll look absolutely beautiful in whatever you choose. You could go up the aisle in a potato sack and would still be the most gorgeous bride ever seen in Cambridge.'

Kate smiled. 'What do you mean Cambridge? What about the rest of the country?' she queried as she sucked in her cheeks while posing in the dressing table mirror.

They both laughed in a shared affection that only a mother and daughter can share.

Kate's mother's absence had allowed Gina and Kate to revert to their most juvenile behaviour and have one of their most hilarious shopping expeditions to date. Not wanting the day to end, Gina agreed to have coffee at Kate's house while they relived every moment. They threw the fruits of their shopping down onto the sofa and Gina smiled at the array of goody bags, pleased that she had bought the whole of her outfit.

'Wasn't that a brilliantly successful day?' She asked rhetorically as she started to unload every bag.

'For some more than others,' Kate shouted out from the kitchen as she made the coffee. 'But just remember, Gina, that unless I get my outfit, yours will be redundant,' she added walking back into the sitting room with the mugs in her hand.

'Well you've got a lovely pair of shoes,' Gina stated. 'And anyway, whose fault is that, Miss Finicky? That last ivory dress you tried on was absolutely stunning.'

'I looked like a bloody serving wench. I'd need a pitcher of ale, not a bouquet, to go with that little concoction.'

'I suppose you're right,' Gina conceded. 'Your cups did overfloweth somewhat, but Max would have loved it! Anyway, enough of that. Do you want to see me in my dress one more time?' she added cheekily.

'Don't push your luck, young lady,' Kate pointed her finger in assumed indignation.

'No? Are you sure?' Gina waved the dress teasingly in front of Kate. 'Shall I take that as a no, then?'

'You'll be wearing something in a minute – this coffee – if you don't shut up and drink yours.'

As they sat in silence for a few moments recalling the day's events, they both laughed at the same time.

'You're remembering that formidable little Italian assistant at 'Delia's Designs' aren't you?' Kate asked almost choking on her drink.

'*Howa dare you saya thatta I'ma forrrrmidable. You no listen to me,*' Gina mimicked with great comic melodrama and exaggerated arm gestures. '*Mama Mia, you signora, you so finnickee. Eeza pity your mama, she havva the flu cos she woulda tella you to putta your brrreasts out.*'

'That's even worse than my Greek accent. Seriously though, I'm not being finicky, really I'm not. I just want the prefect dress. I don't know what it is yet but I will when I see it.'

'And we will find it, my dearest Kate. I promise.'

There was a knock at the door and Kate immediately went to open it. She was surprised to see a tall, dark, attractive man holding up his Police identification.

'Miss Hart?'

'Yes,' replied Kate hesitantly.

'I'm DC Sinclair. Nothing to worry about,' he reassured her with a friendly smile. 'I just need to talk to you about a current case that we think you could help us with.'

'Oh, okay. Please come in,' she gestured for him to sit down.

'She didn't do it officer, honest,' Gina joked as she hurriedly tidied away the shopping and then added, 'I suppose you'd love a pound for every time you heard that one!'

'Not at all, madam,' he replied graciously before turning his attention back to Kate.

'So what can I do for you?' Kate asked, curious as to what this was all about.

'We believe that you could help us regarding a certain Mr. Mikos Kyriakos.'

'Yes I know him but I haven't heard from him for ages. Has something happened to him?' Kate asked. 'By the way, would you like a tea or coffee?'

'No thanks, Miss Hart. Nothing has happened to him. We're gathering evidence to back up possible fraud charges against him and we were given your name by one of the young ladies that he has allegedly defrauded,' DC Sinclair explained as he took out his notebook.

As Kate volunteered the whole story of the how she met Mikos, the night he disappeared and her conversation with Debbie, the officer scribbled down everything he needed to know. He in turn explained that Mikos was up in front of the courts within the next few weeks and that the more evidence they obtained against him, the stronger their case would be. It seemed though that Kate's close escape would spare her the ordeal of being a witness. He concluded by thanking her for her time and that the police would be in touch if they needed her further. Kate was not sure if it was her imagination but he seemed to give Gina an extra special smile as he departed.

CHAPTER 24

'Do you want the good news or the bad news?' Kate asked Gina as they were having lunch in The Plough, a friendly local pub with a reputation for serving good, honest, home made cooking.

'Go on,' Gina replied with a mouthful of fried chicken. 'Surprise me. Something to do with the wedding, perhaps?'

'Oh, I'm not going on about it that much, am I?' Kate asked rhetorically, looking slightly hurt.

'Anyway,' she continued, 'When I was on that Baker day, last Friday, in Huntingdon, I had enough time to go shopping in the lunch hour and guess what? I saw *the* dress, and I mean *the* perfect dress, in a lovely, exclusive bridle shop.'

'So is that the good news or the bad news then?' Gina interrupted but smiled mischievously at her excited friend.

'You're being beastly, Gina you really are. Now, are you going to take this seriously or not?' she admonished, trying not to let the slight hurt she felt show.

'Sorry, I am being a bit horrible but I was only joking. Go on, I'm all ears now. I've finished my food and you have my undivided attention.'

Kate looked intently at Gina and realising that she was being sincere, took a deep breath and proceeded to describe the dress, right down to the last embroidered stitch. 'And I really like it being ivory because, somehow, that is not as hypocritical as wearing white, you know, after everything I've done with Max.'

Gina laughed out loudly, amused by the woman's sudden primness but allowed Kate to finish what she knew would be one of her notorious monologues. 'It fits as though it was made to measure and it really highlights my small waist and also makes me look as well endowed as you. Not only that, I spotted the most adorable pageboy outfit in the world. Kieran will look absolutely scrumptious and as a bonus it's well within my budget. That means that this Saturday's shopping trip will be dedicated to going back there, for Kieran to try it on, if that's okay with you,' she concluded, her eyes brimming with self-satisfaction.

Gina, not wishing to deflate her mood but curious enough to venture forth, hesitated before replying,

'Yes, of course, that's fine by me,' and then leaning forward enquired, 'Now. What bit is the bad news? If anything, it all sounds too good to be true to me.'

'Oh, it's nothing too dramatic really, just a little disappointing, that's all. Max has had a look at our finances and apparently we can't afford a honeymoon, as well as a luxurious wedding, so we've agreed together that we will have a special holiday as soon as we can afford it,' Kate replied wistfully. 'And although my house is sold now we've earmarked that money for our new home and we daren't spend that as we don't know how much we will get for Max's house.'

'Oh, what a shame but you've made the right decision. You can have a holiday anytime but you'll never be able to recreate your wedding day again. Let me buy us another glass of wine to celebrate you finally finding a dress you love. Here's to *the* dress!'

*   *   *   *   *

Max was relaxing in the sitting room when Kate returned from her shopping trip with Gina and Kieran. He had taken advantage of Kate's absence by spending the day playing golf. He had recently taken up the hobby on Kate's insistence that he should unwind at the weekend after a stressful week in the City.

'So how did the round go today?' she asked kissing him on the cheek.

'Bloody embarrassing actually. I didn't par one hole and I came in nine points over my handicap,' he replied sulkily.

'Nine extra points. Isn't that good, then?' Kate looked confused.

Max laughed as he rose out of his chair. 'No, Kate. Less is more in this game. Let's just say, I hope your day was more successful than mine.'

'You'd better believe it,' she replied as she lifted the carrier bags into the air to show him. 'But you can't see the fruits of our labour because, although it's not strictly traditional, I don't want you to get a glimpse of anything to do with the bridal party before the actual day.'

'Please yourself,' Max replied as he switched on the television to catch the football results. 'I've told you before that I'm just happy to turn up on the day.'

'Okay darling. Put the kettle on then, while I pop upstairs to put these away.'

Kate entered the spare room. It was piled high with boxes that contained her belongings, various pieces of stacked furniture and an upended bed, all superfluous to their current needs. On each level surface was a homeless pot plant or an ornament too awkward to be boxed. Amongst all this was a narrow clearing giving just enough access to a wardrobe, which they both used to store the overspill of their bedroom. Kate sighed at the mess, as this was an anathema to her neat and tidy ways. As she opened the wardrobe door so as to quickly hang up her purchases, a waft of air dislodged a slip of paper from the high internal shelf and it floated to the floor. As she bent down to retrieve it, she couldn't help but notice that it was a note from someone called 'Rachael' which read:

"Sorry I couldn't make today. I hope this makes up for it. See you Monday"'

Kate stepped back to view the shelf and apart from the piles of business papers, which Kate laughingly called his filing system, there did not appear to be anything that could be related to this note. Although slightly curious as to who this Rachael was, her attention was soon diverted to the matter in hand which was to hide away all of today's purchases.

*   *   *   *   *

It was not until a week later that 'Rachael' came to her notice again. Kate had worked through her lunch hour preparing for the following day so she could go home early and surprise Max who was working from home. Arriving at the house at 4.30pm she went straight to the back door which she knew Max would have open on such a glorious spring day. As she was about to enter she overheard him on the telephone.

'Actually Rachael, I'm having second thoughts.'

Kate stopped in her tracks as he added,

'No, Kate hasn't got a clue. I just need a bit more time to think things through.'

There was a further pause before he continued. 'Don't worry, I'll find a way to speak to you later.'

Kate stood dumbstruck not knowing which way to turn. Should she enter the house, pretending she hadn't heard anything or should she compose herself first? With her hand over her mouth and the panic rising inside her, she decided to retreat altogether and seek the solace of her best friend. She quietly retraced her steps unnoticed, back to her car, and made her way to Gina's house hoping that she would be home by now. Fortunately Gina was ushering Kieran into the house at the exact moment of her arrival.

Over a coffee Kate described what happened as best she could. Gina waited for her to finish before suggesting a host of possible innocent explanations and managed to calm her down with her logical and gentle approach. Kate agreed that she had jumped to conclusions and decided to return home so that she was no later than Max would be expecting her. As she drove home she felt more composed but couldn't quite eradicate the seed of doubt that was in her mind.

CHAPTER 25

Gina kissed Kieran goodbye at her front door and watched him run excitedly down the path and throw himself into the arms of his waiting father. For the first time in several months, Gina was also looking forward to a Friday evening. Tonight was Kate's hen night and Gina was expecting her at any moment. Once Kieran was out of sight, she skipped her way to the kitchen and wasted no time in pouring two glasses of wine in readiness.

Kate arrived on cue to be welcomed by an animated, shrieking and exhilarated best friend.

'How many of those have you had already?' she asked Gina, as she placed her overnight bag down onto the stairs and accepted the glass of wine that was thrust into her hand.

'This is my first,' Gina replied, slightly affronted by the absence of Kate's sense of occasion. 'This is your hen night, for goodness sake, at least show a little enthusiasm.'

Kate half smiled as she followed Gina into the kitchen and sat down at the table, nurturing her glass of wine.

Gina, still perplexed by the subdued Kate, refused to let the matter drop.

'Is everything alright with Max?' she asked tentatively.

'Oh, It's nothing to do with that,' Kate replied. 'Max has been his normal attentive self and I was just being silly,' she explained, waving her hand as if to dismiss Gina's concern. 'No, I'm feeling a bit nervous, that's all. It's not often a girl has a hen night and I want everyone to remember it for the rest of their lives. And another thing, I'm still not convinced that you or the others haven't planned some excruciatingly embarrassing joke at my expense. So *please* reassure me once more that a half naked man with a huge willy will not be pouncing on me sometime tonight.'

'Kate, my darling. I think you've told me enough times not to get you a kissogram. I wouldn't do anything as crass as that. Don't worry about a thing. I'll look after you and staying here overnight was the best decision you could've made. Who knows what state Max is going to be in after his stag do – but that's the best man's problem. You're mine and I say drink up before the taxi arrives.'

'You're right again, as usual. I have this vision of Max being left naked and trussed up like a chicken, having to hop all the way home. Best I don't even think about it,' she added, pulling a disgusted face.

'Good girl,' Gina laughed. 'Now, let the celebrations begin. This is going to be the hen night of all hen nights.'

* * * * *

Kate sat back in her chair in the steakhouse, chosen especially for it's central location and ability to cater for even the most conservative of palates. She looked around at the group of women celebrating her forthcoming nuptials with her, and acknowledged that she was now beginning to relax. Stephanie, Eloise and her other colleagues, sat furthest away, were making the most noise. Sandie and Claire were ensconced in conversation and Louise, Max's sister was whispering into Stephanie's ear, somewhat mysteriously. However, Kate was not so naïve as to imagine that the whole evening would pass without any surprises and she looked forward to the unknown. Kate's mother was busy gossiping with Gina's mother, about their respective friends. Although these people were unknown to the other, they seemed to find these excessive details of immense interest, which amused both Gina and Kate who felt they were getting a night off from such trivia.

Gina was sitting to her right and was just about to pour herself another glass of wine when her mother stopped herself mid sentence in order to give Gina one of her looks of disapproval.

'Do you really need a third glass of wine?' she asked her daughter.

'Of course she does,' Kate interjected, snatching the bottle from Gina to fill her glass and then her own.

Gina smiled at Kate as she asked, 'Did you know my mum could talk endlessly and count at the same time?'

Kate was about to respond to this gentle sarcasm, when she was given an equally disapproving look from her own mother. Instead she turned to Gina and recommended that they changed the subject before their mothers decided to accompany them to the nightclub after all.

At that moment, there seemed to be some commotion from one end of the table. Stephanie was nudging the others and ushering Louise in the direction of Kate. As Louise started to talk complete nonsense to Kate, it became obvious that this was a ploy to distract her from the figure that was approaching from behind.

Gina turned and then quickly turned back again with an expression of horror.

'Don't look now Kate. I have a feeling that your worst nightmare is behind you but, I assure you, it's got nothing to do with me.'

The entire restaurant paused to watch the scene unfold as a handsome young man, dressed in a white American naval uniform, looking every inch a Richard Gere, began to slowly remove his clothes before handing Kate a bottle of body oil. Kate's embarrassment prevented her from even thinking about touching this complete stranger until Stephanie shouted across the table, 'If you don't give him a rub soon, then give him to me. He cost a fortune and I'm not watching him go to waste.'

Gina's mother surprised everybody by interrupting with her own offer.

'Or perhaps the lovely young man would prefer more experienced hands,' she said turning to face Kate's mother before adding, 'Don't you agree, Sylvia?'

Having been given the unspoken approval of her mother, Kate eagerly poured the oil into her palms and slapped it onto the chest of the gyrating stripper, to the whoops of delight from her party and the other diners. Encouraged by her audience she proceeded to massage his entire torso before being presented with a parting rose. He disappeared out of the door as quickly as he arrived.

Stephanie was quickly forgiven for ignoring Kate's wishes, particularly as this had broken the ice and led to the rest of the evening passing with equally good-natured hilarity.

After settling their mothers into homeward bound taxis, Kate, Gina and the rest of the party moved on to *Bardots*, a tasteful nightclub, renowned for it's hen-night hospitality. Having pre-booked for the occasion, the girls were able to walk in ahead of the queuing guests, and were ushered towards their reserved tables.

Complementary pitchers of Margaritas were served immediately, and with their speedy consumption the revelry began in earnest. There was much laughing, joking and harmless flirting during the course of the evening, punctuated with visits to the dance floor.

When the lights were eventually switched on to indicate it was 2am and time to go home, everyone, particularly Kate, was disappointed that the evening had come to an end.

The stark reality of the well-lit room prompted one of Stephanie's blunt observations.

'God, you lot look rough. No wonder I haven't been able to pull tonight. Who was going to chat me up when I was sitting in the middle of a coven.'

'But Stephanie,' Eloise replied in her slight French accent. 'At least we looked good at the beginning of the evening.'

'Ouch. Touché!'

Once outside and after some very extravagant goodbyes, the party split as the girls went off towards their homes in different directions.

Gina was not as concerned with Kate's alcohol consumption, for this had been moderate, as she was in trying to hail a taxi. Kate was so exhilarated by the success of the evening that she would have been quite happy to walk for hours, chatting and reliving every moment.

She linked arms with Gina, in a show of great affection.

'That was the best hen night ever,' she gushed in her favourite girlie voice. 'And I'm not just saying that because it was mine. Thank you so much for being the best friend a girl could have and looking after me tonight. Well, not just for tonight but also for the last couple of years and, in fact, before that, when we were...'

'Point taken,' Gina interrupted with tolerant humour in her voice. 'I just hope that my matron of honour gift reflects your appreciation.'

This throwaway comment made Kate stop in her tracks as she realised that this was something she had overlooked. She inwardly chastised herself for forgetting such an important part of her responsibility and vowed to rectify it the next morning. At that point she ran after Gina who had managed to procure a taxi.

*   *   *   *   *

The next morning Kate was in town, endeavouring to find the perfect gift for her friend and something special for little Kieran. She could not believe that her organisational skills had let her down so badly and that she had omitted, from any of her numerous lists, any reference to such favours. How could she have been so selfish as to only think of the things that affected her personally?

After some searching, she spotted a beautiful necklace and bracelet set, in the window of a bespoke jeweller, that she knew Gina would adore. She entered the shop and waited patiently to be served while spending some time looking around to see if there was anything for Kieran. When an assistant finally came to serve her, Kate pointed out the set she had noticed. As the assistant was withdrawing the display pad from the window, Kate spotted Max, on the other side of the street, walking passed the shop. She was about to run out to greet him when she was stopped in her tracks as a tall, svelte and stunning woman with long raven hair came into the picture, waving excitedly at Max. Kate's stomach leapt into her mouth as she was reluctantly drawn to the scene unfolding before her. The embrace they shared as they reached each other was far more than a mere friendly greeting and the animated smiles suggested an intimacy beyond camaraderie. Kate's stomach somersaulted, her legs turned to jelly and she was forced to lean against the counter for support as the colour drained from her face.

'Are you feeling okay, madam?' the assistant asked with genuine concern. 'Can I get you some water?' Kate dismissed her. 'No, it's okay, thank-you. I just need some fresh air. I… I'm sorry…' and without finishing her sentence, she walked out of the shop.

Once outside, she scanned the street in both directions but couldn't see any sign of them. With rising panic, she quickly made her way to the spot where she had last seen them but was mortified that they seemed to have disappeared without trace. She stood motionless for a second, as her inner turmoil prohibited her from thinking clearly. With a deep breath and renewed determination, she proceeded to scrutinise the side streets and alleyways in a desperate attempt to find them. The longer her search proved unfruitful, the more she started to find excuses. Was it really Max or just somebody that looked like him? Was it her suspicions about 'Rachael' that had made her see things that weren't there? More fundamentally why, at this point in their relationship, did she not trust Max?

Exhausted and frustrated, she sat down at the nearest street bench to collect her thoughts. The sounds of laughter, chatting and mothers chastising their children echoed distantly in her ears as she tried to make sense of this nightmare. Why were all men unfaithful to her? She had trusted Geoffrey and would have staked her life that he would never have been capable of such a thing. And yet she had been wrong. Mikos was the same and she had been completely taken in by his lies. So, was she so desperate for marriage that Max and his declarations of love had yet again fooled her? It was all fitting into place now – the note from Rachael, the phone call and his reluctance to choose an exotic honeymoon. How could she have been so stupid? He had obviously changed his mind and was about to tell her it was all over. As this realisation dawned on her, her despair reached new depths and she thought her heart would break into tiny pieces. She had to get away completely. She needed time to muster enough strength to face the inevitable. She couldn't confront Max yet and she couldn't face the pity from her friends.

Back home she hurriedly packed a small overnight bag and then rung Gina to explain where she was going and why.

'Are you really sure you want to do this? There could be a perfectly innocent explanation and unless you confront him, you can't be sure.' Gina implored.

'Like what?' Kate almost spat the words out.

'It could just be an old friend he hasn't seen for a while.'

'You weren't there. You didn't see them. It was more than friendship. And what about the note and the phone call? Let's face it Gina, we both know it's Rachael.' Kate was adamant and Gina knew her friend well enough to know that no amount of persuasion would keep her here.

'Well, if that's the way you want to handle this then at least tell me where you're going.'

'I'm going to stay at Sandie's, just for a few days. I'll ring you when I get there.'

Gina had no choice but to reluctantly agree to this course of action but insisted that Kate gave her Sandie's address and telephone number in case she needed to contact her, for whatever reason.

As soon as she put the telephone down from Gina, Kate rang for a taxi to take her to the station. Her short but hair-raising drive home, from the city centre, had proved to Kate that she was in no fit state to drive all the way to Surrey.

*   *   *   *   *

Max and Brandie arrived home after spending several hours shopping. The excitement of seeing each other after several years was now taking its toll and a cup of tea was much needed by the exhausted Max.

'What would you English do without your daily cuppa?' Brandie drawled in her slight Texan accent, as she helped Max unload the car and then added excitedly, 'I can't wait to meet the lovely Kate.'

'Well her car is here so it won't be long before you get the chance.' Max exclaimed proudly.

'I feel as if I know her already. You haven't stopped talking about her all day. Are you sure Kate won't mind me coming over for dinner, without any notice? I can just as easily go back to mums.'

'You'll do no such thing. I haven't had the opportunity to tell her yet but I know she'll love the chance of getting to know her future cousin-in-law,' Max replied as he nodded for Brandie to enter the house.

Max was struck by the silence that greeted him once they were both inside the house. After calling out Kate's name and searching all the rooms, he was completely bewildered by her absence, particularly as her car was parked outside.

Gina was finishing the last of her chores when the telephone rang.

'Gina, it's Max. Is Kate with you?'

Gina paused long enough for Max to realise something was not quite right. She eventually replied.

'No, sorry Max. She isn't,' she responded abruptly, not wanting to lie but trying to give herself enough time to work out what she was going to tell him.

'If you know something Gina then please tell me. I'm frantic with worry. Her car's here and I've been home hours now and there's still no sign of her.'

'I'm not sure I should get involved,' Gina said quietly. 'But I can tell you that she's safe.'

Running his fingers through his hair, Max hesitated for a moment, perplexed by this lack of information. He closed the lounge door, where Brandie was relaxing, to continue with the conversation. He was sure Gina knew more than she was letting on but also recognised that this called for his most delicate powers of persuasion, to find out what on earth was going on.

'If you don't tell me everything you know Gina, then you'll find me on your doorstep within minutes,' Max commanded, trying to suppress the panic in his voice. 'And I won't go away until you do.'

Gina paused for a moment desperately trying to think of the right thing to say. He was obviously out of his mind with worry and she did not feel she could leave him this way.

'Okay, in that case I'll call Kate and ring you back,' Gina relented.

'So you do know where she is. Right, I'm coming round.' Max slammed down the receiver.

Gina dialled the number that she had been given and when Sandie answered, asked if she could speak to Kate urgently. There was a long pause before a dishevelled, red-eyed and listless Kate responded.

'Sorry about this, darling,' Gina apologised. 'But I've just had Max on the phone and he's frantic with worry. He's coming round to find out where you are. What shall I tell him?'

'Tell him anything you like as long as you don't tell him where I am.'

Gina hardly recognised the voice at the other end of the line and decided to seek confirmation.

'Do you really mean that? Do you mean that I can tell him that you know about Rachael?'

'Yes, whatever, I don't really care,' mumbled Kate, as she absent-mindedly straightened the painting hanging on the wall in front of her. 'I trust you to do the right thing.'

Before Gina had a chance to collect her thoughts, Max was at her front door and, to Gina's horror, she could see a young woman waiting in the car. Now it was her turn to be completely baffled. She let him in without saying a word but it didn't matter, as Max needed no invitation to speak.

'No games now Gina. Just tell me where she is and what this is all about,' he demanded.

'You've got a bloody cheek, making demands and acting the innocent victim when Rachael is in the car as we speak,' Gina fired, waving her arm dramatically towards the car.

Max was completely taken aback. 'Who the hell is Rachael?' he screamed emphasising the words with a thrust of his hands.

Gina realised that Max would not be this authentic if he had a guilty secret and that the person in the car, whoever she was, could not be Rachael. The faster the cogs of Gina's mind turned, the further her jaw dropped as slowly she realised that she was in the middle of an escalating misunderstanding and it felt like the equivalent of her own scarab beetle's dung ball.

'Oh, shit!' was all she could reply.

Max placed his hands on Gina's shoulders and gently guided her to the nearest chair, sat her down and asked patiently, 'Right Gina, from the beginning...'

Gina told Max everything he needed to know including where he could find Kate. He in turn explained that the woman in the car was his cousin Brandie, who had flown over from America, secretly, to attend the wedding. She had given him a surprise call that morning and arranged to meet him for lunch.

'And as for Rachael,' he concluded, 'she is my boss' P.A. and was helping me to organise a surprise honeymoon to Hawaii so that I could get the travel agent's discount on the company's account.'

'I'm so sorry, Max. You didn't deserve this but don't be too hard on Kate. She's been hurt badly in the past and couldn't believe her luck when she found you. That, with a bit of wedding nerves thrown into the equation, stopped her from thinking straight.'

Max was calmer now. 'I know and don't worry. I just want to bring her back home.'

'Right, you go now and you needn't worry either. I'll look after Brandie until you get back.'

As soon as Max had left, Gina called Kate and relayed the whole conversation. Kate's initial relief quickly turned to guilt and self-loathing as she took on board the unjustified pain she had put him through. If he could forgive her, she would never doubt him again. By the time Max reached his destination, Kate was waiting at the window and rushed out to greet him. She flung her arms around his neck, apologising profusely.

'Oh my poor darling Max. I am so, so sorry. Can you ever forgive me? I'll never doubt you again, I promise,' she wept into his neck.

Max took her face between his hands, looked at her intently and implored, 'Don't ever leave me again,' and before she could reply, he kissed her more fervently than ever before.

CHAPTER 26

It was in the most glorious Easter sunshine that Gina waited, under the dappled shade of the majestic willow tree that stood outside the church. She surveyed her surroundings, watching the guests in all their kaleidoscopic glory, as they gathered to share in Max and Kate's day.

Gina looked down at her own beautifully made, aubergine satin gown with her matching shoes and posy of cream roses and imagined how Matt would have reacted, had he been with her today. She felt a bittersweet, warm glow as she could almost sense his presence.

She looked over at Kieran, who was practically standing to attention, having taken too seriously her warning not to get dirty before the ceremony. His deep purple velvet jacket and knickerbockers gave him an air of importance over all the other children and this was all the more evident as Gina spotted him nodding to the guests as they walked by. Gina could not help being overwhelmed as she was reminded that her special day, with Kieran as her own pageboy, had been cruelly snatched from her. She pushed her thoughts to the back of her mind and continued to take in the scene.

The two future mother-in-laws were surreptitiously eyeing each other up and down, comparing outfits. One was pale lilac and the other corn flour blue but, save for the colour, Gina could not notice any other difference between the two. And yet they continued to scrutinise each other, right down to the last feather in their hats, until they inadvertently caught each other's eye and were forced to share an embarrassed smile.

Max was pacing nervously near the church entrance, only moving away once to join a group of his friends to share a furtive cigarette while discussing the possible outcome of that afternoon's match. Gina noted how formal attire made him look even more upstanding than he normally did and his natural apprehension, as he continually looked at his watch, made Gina smile inwardly. At one point one of his friends patted him on the back and obviously made a joke at his expense as all the members of the group laughed heartily.

Nearby, Stephanie and Kate's other friends were eyeing up the talent and giggling flirtatiously. Moreover, this farcical attempt to attract their attention proved wholly successful as the men started to showcase their own virtues, in response. Brandie and Louise looked on enviously because the two cousins had been unable to escape the clutches of their adoring mothers, who talked endlessly about the girls and their exploits when they were young.

Three of Kate's aunts walked by, gossiping about various members of the family.

'He never?' Gina just managed to catch, along with the reply, 'Oh, yes he did!'

Gina tried, but never did establish who he was or what he'd done, especially as, at that moment, there was a shout from the best man that the bridal car was coming up the road. He ushered everybody into the church, except for Gina and Kieran who waited to perform their duties.

As Kate emerged from the car, assisted by her proud father, Gina could feel the tears welling up in her eyes and made a conscious effort to not let them ruin her perfectly applied make up. Although Gina had seen the dress before, she could not believe how dazzling Kate looked, wearing the entire ensemble. The ivory satin dress was finished perfectly by matching satin pumps and a garland of cream roses in her hair, which echoed the bridal bouquet. Gina leant forward to kiss her friend and whispered into her ear, 'You look magnificent, my darling. You're going to knock him dead.' Then taking her hand, she looked purposefully into her eyes and added, 'Kate, please savour *every* moment.'

Gina and Kieran then took their place behind Kate as the organist began playing the glorious chords of a wedding fanfare.

As Gina followed her up the aisle and she caught a glimpse of the biggest smile on Kate's face, her hand stroked her growing tummy as she acknowledged that it was not only Kate who had a new beginning.

THE END